Suddenly Alison's eyes opened wide. Her fingers bit into my arm. "Carly! I hear something!" she whispered. "Someone's following us!"

We both froze. I could hear rustling behind us. Someone was coming!

Alison pulled me behind the nearest bushes. We crouched down, hugging each other. I could smell the muck on her sneakers.

"At least whoever's coming isn't driving a tractor," I whispered.

She nodded, but her face was chalky. We should have waited until Randy could come, I told myself. No one else knew we were here. If something happened . . .

The Secret of Seaside

Linda Barr

To my son Dan, who is now finishing his degree in environmental engineering and will soon be helping to find more "secrets" like the one at Seaside.

Many thanks to Ron Meyers, Program Director for the Columbus, Ohio office of Ohio Citizens Action Group, and his staff. They helped with the extensive research that underlies *The Secret of Seaside*.

Published by Willowisp Press
801 94th Avenue North, St. Petersburg, Florida 33702

Copyright © 1995 by Willowisp Press,
a division of PAGES, Inc.

Printed in the United States of America

2 4 6 8 10 9 7 5 3 1

ISBN 0-87406-746-4

One

WALK slower, I told myself. And stop biting your lip. Pretend you're just looking around the new park, seeing what's here. Maybe no one will figure out you're actually searching for the little boy you were supposed to be baby-sitting!

For the fourth or fifth time, I glanced over at the big square sandbox, the last place I had seen Jeremy. Two giggling boys were still sitting in the middle of it, tossing sand at each other. All that was left of Jeremy was the damp hole he had been digging.

Where had he gone? I tried to block out the laughing and squealing of the kids on the park swings so I could concentrate.

The park had been carved out of the woods in a new part of Seaside, five or six blocks from Jeremy's house. Tall pines framed the sides and back of the park. A cluster of trees in the middle shaded the wooden sandbox, three swings, and a wooden bench. The front of the park faced a street so new it didn't have a name yet.

At least Ginny seemed to be too busy to notice I had lost her son. She was standing near the street now, talking with the mayor of Seaside and some other people in suits. Two men were unloading folding chairs from a van and putting them in rows on the grass. It was almost time for the official ceremony to open the park.

But where was Jeremy? I had to find him before he got hurt somehow. I searched the park again, praying to find a little boy with straight blond hair and a blue-and-red striped shirt.

No luck. As best I could tell, Jeremy had disappeared!

A cold lump formed in the pit of my stomach. I glanced at Ginny again. Now she was showing the mayor some papers.

Ginny didn't expect you to lose her son, I told myself. That's why she isn't checking to make sure he's still with you. She trusts you to take care of him! The cold lump grew bigger.

"Jeremy!" I wanted to yell. "Where are you? You're scaring me to death!"

Ever since January, right after Dad and I

moved to Seaside from Indianapolis, I had been baby-sitting Jeremy three afternoons a week while Ginny worked. She was a real estate agent. That's how Dad and I met her— she sold us our house. When school ended for the summer over two weeks ago, Ginny had asked me to take care of Jeremy every morning.

Dad wanted me to take the job because he thought I'd be lonely at home by myself. My mom had died in a car accident when I was a baby. I hadn't made many friends in Seaside yet, and I'd been dreading the empty summer days ahead, so I jumped at the chance to baby-sit Jeremy in the mornings. He and I usually had a good time together.

But this was torture! I took a deep breath and tried to relax the muscles in my face so I wouldn't look as panicked as I felt. Where was he? Had he tried to walk home by himself? Did he even know how to get there?

Just then car brakes screeched somewhere close. My breath caught in my throat. Had Jeremy been hit?

As I stumbled toward the street on rubbery legs, a little voice behind me called, "Carly, come and see the water!"

Jeremy! I swiveled and saw him dash into the woods that lined the back of the park.

Thank goodness he was okay!

"Jeremy, wait! Wait!" I hurried after him and plunged into the thick wall of trees and bushes where he had disappeared—and nearly stepped right into a shallow stream. It was almost hidden by a tangle of bushes.

Jeremy was kneeling on the narrow bank, trailing his hand in the rippling water. "See? A lake! I finded it all by myself!"

"Jeremy! You're too little to find anything by yourself!"

He frowned up at me. His blond bangs nearly hid his big blue eyes. "Mommy says I'm a big boy now!" He held up four fingers to remind me how old and wise and experienced he was.

I sighed. At least he was safe.

Then he put his face close to the water and called, "Fishies? Where are you, fishies?"

I walked over to help him look, but nothing moved in the clear water. I grabbed a stick and poked at some stones. I thought a tadpole or crayfish might run out, but nothing happened. Maybe it was the wrong time of the year for them.

The sound of people clapping filtered through the trees.

"The ceremony's starting!" I said, tossing my stick in the water. "Let's go watch Mommy!"

"Okay!" Jeremy smacked the water with his hand, then giggled when it splattered his shorts and shirt.

Mayor Haynes was talking when we pushed back through the trees into the sunshine. Jeremy didn't care what the mayor had to say, even about his mom, so he trotted back to the sandbox. I sat on the edge of the sandbox, close enough to touch him, so I could watch the ceremony without losing him again.

Ginny was standing beside the mayor and smiling at the audience—our neighbors and their kids and a few people in suits.

"Without Ginny Newman," Mayor Haynes told the small crowd, "we wouldn't have this park!"

He was right about that. Ginny had told me the park was her present to all the people she had helped find houses in our neighborhood. She had been a real estate agent only three years, since her divorce, and I knew she really cared about her "customers." Ginny had talked the company that built our houses into donating land for the park. She had also talked Faraday Fuel Corporation into paying for the swings and sandbox and bench. Most of the people in Seaside worked at Faraday, including my dad.

Just then, I saw Alison standing near the

sidewalk, looking around the park. I waved and she hurried over. We'd been best friends since March, when we did a book report together in English class. Today she had on her "Save the Whales" shirt.

"I've been taking notes on the mayor's speech for you," I whispered to her. "I knew you wouldn't want to miss a word."

"Oh, sure!" She rolled her eyes and tucked a strand of long brown hair behind her ear. "Want an apple?" She handed a small apple to each of us.

"Is it 'ganic?" Jeremy asked.

"'Course!" she said. "But you say it 'organic,' you know. Remember what that means?"

"Yeah! No poison, right?"

Alison had told him insecticides were poison.

"That's right," I said. "No poison, just worms."

Jeremy's eyes flew open and he dropped his apple in the sandbox.

"Carly Hendricks, quit that!" Alison brushed the sand off the apple and handed it back to him. "No worms, either! I checked and everything."

She stuck her tongue out at me, but I just grinned. Jeremy looked the apple over and took a big bite.

"Didn't Randy start his new job yesterday?" Alison asked me. "I mean, how's he doin'?"

Randy was the closest thing I'd ever had to a boyfriend. He was sixteen so he had a real summer job—at Faraday, of course. Faraday processed fuel for airplanes. Randy was supposed to work every afternoon in the warehouse, moving boxes around.

I shrugged. "He hasn't called, so I don't know."

"Carly, call *him!* Girls are allowed to use the phone too, you know!"

That was easy for her to say. Alison didn't have one special boyfriend right then, but she was friends with lots of guys and called them whenever she felt like it.

I, on the other hand, had watched Randy on the school bus and in my algebra class for two months without saying a word to him. I liked his lopsided smile and the way his hair was the same blondish brown as mine and nearly as curly.

Then one morning I was rushing to finish my algebra on the bus before we got to school. The seventh problem had me stumped. I noticed Randy sitting two seats in front of me, and—without thinking—I reached over and tapped him on the shoulder.

"Randy, did you get seven?"

He turned and gave me a confused look.

11

"Seven what?" he asked.

My cheeks started to burn. Oh, no! He didn't even know I was in his algebra class!

I held up my worksheet to hide my face.

"Oh, algebra!" I heard him say. "I got 'em all. I'll come back and show you."

I practically hopped into Alison's lap when Randy crowded into the seat with us. When we got to school, I couldn't remember a thing he had said.

Then a couple of days later, Randy got off the bus at my stop and walked me home. I couldn't believe it!

"Where's Alison?" he asked.

I tried to keep smiling. After all, lots of guys liked Alison. Including Randy, it seemed.

"At a meeting," I told him. "She and some other kids are trying to get the school cafeteria to give us organic fruits and vegetables instead of so much greasy pizza."

"How come you aren't at the meeting?" he asked. "I thought you and Alison were always together."

Randy had been watching me! I started to blush until I remembered he said "you and Alison." Forget it, I told myself. He's watching Alison.

"Uh . . . I kind of like greasy pizza, so I didn't go," I mumbled.

Randy nodded. "The cafeteria pizza's not too bad. At least no one ever died from eating it, right?"

"I guess not," I told him. "But I've only lived in Seaside a few months. Maybe some kids died before Dad and I moved here."

He grinned. I was admiring how his blue eyes crinkled at the corners when he said, "So how about going to a movie with me on Friday?"

My cheeks started to heat up again. What about Alison?

"I promise to buy you some nice greasy popcorn," he added.

"Well, since you put it that way . . . " He really meant me!

We had a great time at the movie, even though we had to take the city bus because Dad didn't trust Randy's driving. Randy walked me home from the school bus stop once or twice a week after that, usually on days when Alison stayed at school for meetings.

Jeremy brought me back down to earth. He was tugging on Alison's hand. "Come and see my lake!"

"Lake?" she asked.

"Jeremy found a stream behind those trees." I pointed toward the back of the park. "Want to see it?"

"Oh, I really do, but I've got to baby-sit Cecily now. Show me tomorrow, Jere, okay? See you later, Carly!" Alison waved and hurried off.

The ceremony was over now. The people in suits had left and the neighbors and their children had drifted around the park. Ginny was still talking to the mayor.

"Look, Carly!" Jeremy had found a red plastic sand bucket. "A boat for the lake!"

"Let's try it out."

We pushed back through the bushes that hid the stream. Jeremy walked a little way up the bank and set his bucket-boat in the water. It floated down the stream, bumping against rocks and almost tipping twice. It stopped against a tree root that had grown into the water.

Jeremy squealed with delight. "I do it again." He started toward the stream to get the bucket.

"Wait!" I grabbed his arm. "Take your shoes off."

He plopped down on the bank and yanked off his sneakers and socks while I peered into the water again. I still didn't see any fish, but I couldn't see any glass or rusty nails either. Even the rocks had smooth edges. Anyway, it didn't seem likely anyone had thrown broken bottles or old cans into this stream. I bet most people didn't even know it was here.

Jeremy waded in, giggling as the water tickled his feet. In the middle, it came only halfway to his knees. He retrieved the bucket, climbed out, and ran back upstream to sail it again.

I sat on the bank and listened to the water trickle over the stones in its path. The trees on both banks met high overhead, a lacy ceiling on a shady cave.

Maybe tomorrow morning, I thought, Jeremy and I could bring a snack and have a picnic here.

The only thing out of place was a slight smell. At first I thought it was the tiny blue flowers that grew in sunny spots on the far bank. Only it didn't smell like flowers. Maybe someone had put insecticide or a chemical fertilizer on the new grass in the park. Alison would have a fit!

Two

WHEN I got to Jeremy's house Monday morning, he was on the floor giggling as an excited little dog licked his entire face. One of Ginny's clients had given her a puppy.

"Freckles! Stop!" Jeremy managed to say between giggles.

"Freckles?" Then I noticed the splatter of brown spots on the dog's white fur. Freckles stopped slobbering on Jeremy for a minute and looked up at me with big brown eyes. Her ears hung down beside her face. She was adorable.

"I hope you don't mind, Carly," Ginny said. "Jeremy has promised to help take care of her." Then she winked to tell me she knew how much help he would be.

Jeremy did know how to fasten the leash on Freckles' collar, and he insisted on taking her everywhere. Monday and Tuesday we spent a lot of time at the new park and the stream—mostly because there was no rug for cute, cuddly Freckles to wet on.

Wednesday it rained, so while Freckles napped in her basket on the kitchen floor, I let Jeremy finger-paint at the kitchen table. Afterward, while I was rinsing him off at the sink, I noticed a pink rash on the inside of his left elbow. I quickly looked at his right arm. It was there, too.

"Does Mommy know about this, Jeremy?"

He answered my question by staring at the little pink spots.

"Is that a boo-boo?"

"Not exactly, honey. Does it itch?"

"Uh . . . " He peered closely at his arm. "Nope!"

"How do you feel?"

"Hungry!"

Nothing new there. Jeremy's stomach didn't hurt, that was clear. I felt his forehead, but it was nice and cool.

So where did the rash come from? I told Ginny about it as soon as she got home. She found more spots behind Jeremy's knees.

"I don't know what it is," she told me with a frown. "Did you see any poison ivy in the park or by that stream?" She had already visited the stream at Jeremy's insistence.

"No," I said, "but I'll look again."

She nodded. "Let's just wait and check him tomorrow. Those spots will probably be gone by then."

The next morning I didn't even remember the rash. We went to the park so Jeremy could dig in the sandbox. The day was so hot and muggy that even Freckles was lying in the shade, panting.

"Carly, I cooked some soup for you." Jeremy grinned as he lifted up a spoonful of sand for me to taste. That's when I noticed the spots inside his elbow again. Sand was sticking to the damp creases, so I couldn't see whether the rash was getting better.

"Let's go rinse off in the stream," I suggested.

"Okay! C'mon, Freckles!"

They raced toward the back of the park. I grabbed the plastic boat Ginny had bought for Jeremy and started after them.

"Hey, Carly! Wait up!"

I turned toward the familiar voice. Alison had dropped her bike on the grass and was hurrying over.

Today she was wearing Jeremy's favorite shirt, the one picturing a baby seal with huge eyes. Below the picture it said "Save me!" We didn't tell Jeremy what the words meant.

"Hi, Alison!" I said. "Come on back to the stream with us." Then I remembered. "Ginny wants me to check for poison ivy. You can help."

"Just so I don't, you know, touch any." Alison rubbed the backs of her hands.

Jeremy pulled off his sneakers and socks at the bank of the stream. I helped him get his shirt off. He and Freckles splashed around while Alison and I searched for poison ivy.

Actually, Alison just stood near the stream and glanced around. She wasn't taking chances on touching any plant she didn't recognize.

I looked under the bushes and around the trees. "If there's poison ivy here, I sure can't find it."

"Good!" Alison eased herself onto the bank. I sat down beside her, and we watched Jeremy and Freckles get soaking wet.

Then I had an interesting thought. "Maybe I should bring Randy here," I whispered to Alison. "Do you think he would kiss me?"

"Maybe . . . but, I mean, what would Jeremy think?"

"Alison! I—we—wouldn't kiss in front of him!"

Then she grinned.

"This isn't funny! Here I am planning my first kiss and you're making jokes!"

Alison reached over and hugged me. "Sorry, Carly!"

I could feel her body shake with smothered giggles, but I pretended not to notice. I needed her advice. I was nervous even thinking about kissing Randy, but I still wanted to try it—if he did.

Randy hadn't kissed me when we went to the movies, of course. But just last week he had ridden his bike past Ginny's house while Jeremy and I were playing catch in the front yard. Didn't that prove he liked me a little? Or was he totally surprised to see me there? I hoped not.

"Hey, Carly!" he had yelled.

"Hi!" I tried to comb the tangles out of my hair with my fingers, but it was hopeless. "How's your job going?"

He stopped his bike by the curb and leaned on the handlebars. "Working in the warehouse is okay, but next summer will be a lot better. I've got a good chance of being a gofer in Faraday's engineering department."

"A gopher?" He was kidding, right?

Randy chuckled. "A 'gofer.' You know—go fer blueprints, go fer coffee. A helper."

"Oh." My cheeks started to burn.

Randy smiled. Had he been thinking about kissing me? With my luck, he'd been thinking about being a gofer.

"This *is* a good place for a kiss, though,

20

don't you think?" I asked Alison. "With no one else around?"

"Maybe, maybe not." Alison gestured toward an area across the stream. "I mean, what about Betty and Joe?"

She was looking past the trees on the other side of the stream, across a wide, weedy field. At the far edge of the field stood an old wooden farmhouse. Its white paint had turned yellow from years in the sun. Behind the house, a reddish barn was nearing collapse. Its big double doors hung open, and even from this distance, I could see that its roof sagged dangerously low in the middle.

"I forgot about Betty and Joe," I admitted.

Betty and Joe Robbins, brother and sister, had lived in that farmhouse since long before our neighborhood was built.

The wide front porch of the farmhouse faced us. One end was hidden by a faded red pickup truck parked in the dirt yard. At the other end of the porch, Betty was sitting on a swing. I could make out a little cart beside the swing, and knew it was for her oxygen tank. She was really sick, I had heard, and had to pull the oxygen tank around with her everywhere she went.

"I wonder if she likes having the park here," I said.

Alison shrugged. "Maybe. Maybe she liked it better, you know, when all this land was still her family farm. I mean, her brother did, for sure."

Alison had told me how Joe almost scared her to death one day before I moved to Seaside. She had wandered onto his farm looking for wildflowers, and he had chased her off with a huge tractor.

"I bet Betty wouldn't have chased you away," I said. "She was a teacher once, wasn't she? She must like people a little, even if Joe doesn't."

"Yeah, but you know what the kids at school say about her," Alison said.

"You mean about her face?"

The kids told sickening stories about Betty's face. I wasn't sure how much was true, but I knew she wasn't pretty.

Alison nodded and hugged herself. "How can she, you know, stand all those blisters and everything?"

"Maybe she didn't always look that way." I splashed some water on my arms and legs to cool off. "I wonder if anyone ever comes to see her. Do you think Joe chases adults away, too?"

"Probably. I mean, I can just see him mowing down some little old ladies with his

22

tractor. They can't run very fast, you know."

I smiled. "There are laws against that, Alison."

She shrugged. "There must be a law against running down girls, too, you know, but Joe sure didn't seem worried about it when he went after me. Anyway, someone told me Joe's got sores on his face, too."

Jeremy was wading behind his boat as it floated down the stream. Freckles splashed along beside him, nipping at the boat.

"I wonder why Joe and Betty both have those sores," I said.

"I bet it's some family disease or something."

"Maybe. Betty sure looks lonely."

Her swing was still now. Maybe she had fallen asleep.

I glanced at my watch. It was nearly noon. "Oops! We gotta go. Ginny'll be home in a few minutes."

While I snapped the leash on Freckles, Alison helped Jeremy put his shirt back on. At least that was dry.

"Uh-oh, Jeremy!" she said. "Looks like you're the one who found the poison ivy or something!" She was holding his arm out, being very careful not to touch his rash.

Now I could see that the rash had spread from the inside of his elbow nearly up to his arm pit and down to his wrist. On the other arm, too. And it had spread further up and down the backs of his legs. The oldest spots were an angry red.

"He had this yesterday," I told Alison, "but it wasn't this bad. I don't think it's poison ivy, since we didn't find any."

I felt Jeremy's forehead again. It was still cool, but his eyes were red-rimmed and his nose was running.

When Ginny saw how Jeremy's rash had spread, she made a doctor's appointment for the next day, Friday. She called me that afternoon as soon as they got back.

"Dr. Graves thinks Jeremy is mildly allergic to animal fur."

"Freckles?"

Ginny sighed. "I guess so. He prescribed some pills and cream that should help. I hope they work so we can keep her."

They better work, I thought. Jeremy would rather give up his skin than Freckles.

* * * * *

Monday morning at the park, Jeremy tried to build a dam across the stream, using rocks and his hands and feet to stop the water. He giggled when the water kept sneaking through the cracks.

When it was time to go, I got out the tube of cream that the doctor had prescribed. Jeremy's rash looked redder than ever, and some spots had spread to his stomach and face. Gently, I applied the cream to them. Jeremy winced a little when I touched the worst places.

I gave him a tissue for his runny nose, but I couldn't do anything about his red-rimmed eyes. Poor kid.

So far the cream and pills weren't doing much good, but it had only been three days. I still had my fingers crossed, for Freckles' sake—and Jeremy's.

"There you are!" Cecily shouted, bursting through the trees and shattering the quiet. I jumped about a foot and wondered for the hundredth time if she ever talked in a normal voice.

"Cecily, I said wait for me!" Alison called out as she pushed through the trees.

Five-year-old Cecily, little curls circling her face, hurried over and gave Jeremy a bear hug.

"Be careful, Cecily!" I warned. But she had already smeared some of Jeremy's cream on her arms.

"Yuck!" she yelled at the top of her lungs. She held her arms out as if they were suddenly the most disgusting things in the world. "Look what you did, Jeremy! You're icky!"

Jeremy looked at his own whitened arms. "I am not icky!" His lower lip started to tremble.

"It's okay, honey." I patted his shoulder.

But Cecily was merciless. "What's wrong with you, Jeremy?"

"Ah, Cecily, dearest . . . " Alison grabbed the little girl's arm and pulled her back through the trees. "Let's go home. I hear your mom calling us, you know."

"I don't!" Cecily insisted.

Alison looked at me and rolled her eyes. "Sorry, Carly. I'll call you later, okay?"

As they disappeared, Jeremy's face got as dark as a thunder cloud. "I don't want this icky stuff on me!" He wiped one arm on his shorts.

"Wait! The cream will help your skin! You have to keep it on or . . . " Or Freckles is history, I almost blurted out. "C'mon, sweetie, let's go home and have lunch."

The thunder cloud lifted a little. "Oh . . . okay."

We waited while Freckles took a long drink out of the stream. Then we headed home. We were almost there when Freckles threw up on the sidewalk.

Now it was Jeremy who yelled, "Yuck!"

I looked at the two of them. Freckles sat beside the mess on the sidewalk with her head drooping. Jeremy stood beside her with his hand over his mouth and his skin glistening with cream. For a second, I wished I were old enough to work at Faraday. It had to be easier.

I pushed Jeremy's damp hair out of his eyes. "Freckles must not feel good today. We'll walk slower so she can keep up."

We'd only gone a few steps, though, when Freckles started coughing, as if she might throw up again.

"Don't worry, Freckles," Jeremy said softly. "I carry you. You're sick."

He started to pick her up. Freckles gave me a pleading look.

"Wait, Jeremy. I think Freckles would rather walk." I unwrapped his arms from the poor dog and tried to wipe his cream off her fur.

"You carry me when I'm sick," Jeremy reminded me.

"That's true, honey, but dogs like to walk," I said, making no sense at all.

Fortunately, Jeremy nodded and we continued on home. Ginny was already there.

"Mommy, Freckles barfed!" Jeremy announced.

Ginny looked at me and I shrugged. Freckles walked over to her basket and lay down with her head on her paws.

Ginny reached down and smoothed Freckles' fur. "Poor baby." Freckles wagged her tail a little, but she didn't raise her head.

Then Ginny turned to her son. "Let's see how you're doing."

Uh-oh, I thought.

Ginny frowned as she checked his arms and legs. Then she said, "Jeremy, aren't your cartoons on now?"

"Yeah!" He ran into the family room. Seconds later, the TV was blaring a cereal commercial.

She turned to me. "That rash looks even worse than it did *before* we went to the doctor."

"I know."

Ginny leaned closer. "I hope Freckles isn't really sick. I already called the family who gave her to us. I told them we might have to give her back. Now I'm sure we do."

As if Freckles understood she would be leaving soon, she slowly climbed out of her basket and padded into the family room to be with Jeremy.

I shut my eyes. It just didn't seem fair.

Ginny sighed. "Carly, could you eat lunch

with us and then stay while Jeremy takes his nap? I'll take Freckles over then."

That's how we did it. I went home as soon as Ginny got back, before Jeremy woke up. I didn't want to be there when she told him what happened to Freckles. I wasn't sure a four-year-old would understand about allergies.

But I tried to be optimistic. Next week Jeremy and his mom were going to visit his grandparents in Connecticut. By the time they returned, maybe he would have forgotten about Freckles—or at least not feel quite so sad. His rash might clear up by then, too. We could kind of start the summer over.

And maybe I could buy another boat for the stream. Jeremy's old one leaked where Freckles had chewed it. It would be like a "welcome home" present when they got back.

Three

SUNDAY night Randy called. I nearly dropped the phone when I heard his voice.

"How's the baby-sitting going?" he asked.

I was so nervous I started talking and couldn't stop. I told him about Jeremy's rash and poor Freckles and Jeremy visiting his grandparents and . . .

Finally Randy interrupted me. "Since you don't have to baby-sit, maybe we could do something tomorrow. If you want to."

Did I! I was so excited by the time we hung up I could hardly dial Alison's number.

"That's great!" she said. "Has he seen the stream yet?"

Then she giggled and I remembered talking about the stream being a good place for my first kiss. I lay awake for hours that night, thinking about the possibilities.

I had been ready for about two hours by

the time Randy rang our doorbell at ten. He had on a deep blue shirt that matched his eyes. And he smelled wonderful.

"Want to walk to the park?" he asked.

"The park?" Could he read my mind?

He gave me a puzzled look. "You know—the new park?"

"Oh, that one? Sure!" Then I giggled.

He gave me another puzzled look, but I just smiled.

Randy had been to the park before, but when I led him through the trees to the stream, he was definitely surprised. He stood with his hands in his back pockets, looking around.

"This is great! We had a stream like this behind the house where we used to live. Kids were always in our backyard, building dams and looking for frogs and turtles and other stuff."

Then he grinned. "Want to catch some frogs, Carly?"

I wouldn't have minded, just to stay near him, but I shrugged. "I can't. I left my frog net at home."

He laughed and reached over to pull me closer. I felt his arm around my waist and my heart almost stopped! This was it!

Just then a motor roared nearby. Both of us

jumped a foot and Randy let go of me.

The roar was coming from across the stream. The old red pickup was bumping down the farmhouse's rutted driveway. I could see a man, probably Joe, driving.

I was sure Randy had been getting ready to kiss me! I felt like crying, but I tried to pretend nothing was wrong. "Do you know Joe and Betty?" I asked.

He shook his head. "My family has lived here about a year, but Joe and Betty haven't asked us over once."

I smiled and glanced over at the farmhouse to see if Betty was sitting on the porch. The porch was empty, but . . .

"What's that?" I pointed. "There, in the middle of the field!" Something small and brownish was moving toward us.

Randy squinted into the sun. "A rabbit, I guess."

But it wasn't hopping like a rabbit.

"I think it's a kitten!" I looked for rocks I could step on to get across the stream.

"What are you . . . ?" Randy asked.

But I was already on the other side. "Kitty, kitty, kitty?" I called as I started into the field.

"Carly, wait . . . "

I heard splashing behind me as the kitten came closer.

"Randy, it's a little orange kitten!"

I hurried toward the little animal and picked her up. She was as light as a leaf, but she purred and rubbed her head against me as I carried her back to Randy. He was standing beside the stream with wet sneakers and his hands on his hips.

"Carly, that cat looks sick," he said.

"She's okay. She just needs something to eat. I wonder who . . . " I glanced back across the field. Betty was standing on her porch now, shading her eyes with one hand as she looked across the field. Searching for her kitten, no doubt.

"I bet it's Betty's," I said to Randy. Darn! I was already planning what I would feed the skinny little cat when I got her home. "I guess we should take her back."

"Just put it down. It'll go back."

"Maybe not." I scratched the top of the cat's head. She meowed at me. "She's awfully little, Randy. Maybe she doesn't know how to get back. And Betty sure can't pull her oxygen tank through this field, looking for her."

"Carly—"

"Anyway, Joe isn't even there right now."

"What difference does that make?"

I shrugged. "None, really." No point in telling him about Joe chasing Alison.

33

Randy glanced at his watch. "I have to go to work pretty soon."

"This will only take a minute." I grinned up at him. I sure wasn't going to stay long. No telling when Joe would be back.

Randy just stood there studying the weedy field, so I tucked the kitten under one arm, grabbed his hand, and started picking my way through the weeds.

Behind me, Randy muttered, "You're nuts, you know. I'm just doing this to humor you."

"You won't be sorry!" As long as Joe doesn't come back, I reminded myself.

Halfway across, I looked up and saw Betty watching us from the porch. I smiled and waved. She raised her hand slowly. I knew she was probably surprised to see us. She was wearing a faded house dress. I could see the little cart beside her.

"She's sure going to be glad we brought her kitten back," I said to encourage Randy.

"Mmm," was all he offered.

About the time we reached the dirt yard, an odor kind of burned my nose. I'd smelled something like it before, but where?

"Oh! Oh my . . . ," Betty murmured as Randy and I started up the splintered porch steps. She reached out to take her kitten before we were close enough to give it to her. But we were plenty close enough to see her face.

Don't look away, I told myself.

The kids at school hadn't been exaggerating.

Betty's face was a teenager's nightmare, full of small pimples, bigger blisters, and dark scabs. Her wispy white hair was so thin I could see more sores and scabs on her scalp.

A plastic tube ran across her face, just under her nose. It seemed to hook over her ears on both sides, like eyeglasses. Another tube led from under her nose to the oxygen tank.

Her thin hands were dotted with more blisters and scabs. In fact, most of her skin was red, as if she'd been burned. Is *that* what happened, I wondered.

"Hi," I said in a strangled voice. "This is Randy and I'm Carly. We live over there." I waved toward the park and the houses beyond it.

Betty was cuddling the kitten, who didn't seem to mind her blisters. She rubbed against Betty's thin chest and meowed up at her. "There, there, Sweetie," she told the cat in a wheezy voice. "You're . . . you're safe now."

Then Betty looked at us. Her light blue eyes were kind, but red-rimmed and watery. "Well, well . . . thank you. Thank you . . . for bringing Sweetie back."

"Uh, that's okay," I managed to say.

At least Randy was thinking. "Do you want to sit down?" he asked Betty.

The woman nodded and took two unsteady steps to the porch swing, clutching her kitten with one hand and pulling the cart with the other. Randy put his hand under her elbow and eased her down on the seat.

Betty fumbled with one of the plastic pieces that had slipped off her ear. Finally she got it hooked back on. I could hear something rattle in her chest every time she breathed.

"Uh . . . that sure is a cute kitten," I said.

Betty smiled and hugged its thin body. "I . . . I don't know . . . what I'd do without . . . without Sweetie."

I figured Joe wasn't much company.

"Well . . . " Randy moved toward the porch steps, but I wasn't ready to go. I remembered how lonely Betty had looked, sitting by herself on this swing for hours.

"Um, didn't you used to teach at Seaside High?" I sat down on the swing beside her.

Randy gave me an impatient look, but he stayed where he was.

Betty stopped petting the cat and looked at me. "Why, yes. Were you . . . ?"

Then she shook her head and started to laugh, but her breath caught in her throat. She pulled a dingy handkerchief out of her pocket and made little coughing, choking sounds into it.

Randy met my eyes. I'm sure I looked as worried as he did. I considered pounding her on the back, but she seemed too fragile for that.

"Need some help?" I tried to keep my voice steady.

She shook her head a little as she struggled to breathe.

Finally she gave one loud cough and seemed to spit something up. She closed the handkerchief around it and put the wad back in her pocket. I swallowed hard. At least now she was able to breathe easier.

"I thought . . . " She cleared her throat and smiled a little, as if nothing had happened. "I thought . . . you . . . " She shook her head. "But that was . . . so long . . . so long ago. You're too . . . too young." She patted my arm.

Then I understood. "You thought maybe we were in one of your classes?"

Betty nodded and kept smiling. "What a . . . what a foolish old . . . lady . . . I am."

Maybe it was her smile, but for some reason she didn't look so scary anymore. I wished we *had* been in her class. I stole a look at Randy. He was smiling, too.

"How long ago did you teach at Seaside?" he asked.

"Oh . . . let's see." Betty coughed a little. I could hear something rattle in her chest again. I crossed my fingers she wouldn't have more trouble.

"It was . . . about . . . " She stared out into the front yard as she thought. I wondered how long it had been since anyone had asked about her teaching. Maybe, I thought, no one but Joe had even talked to her for years.

"I taught at . . . at Seaside till about . . . oh, about fifteen or so years . . . ago. Then I . . . got too sick. I hear they even . . . built . . . a new . . . high school."

New? That school had to be nearly as old as I was! But Betty hadn't even seen it. How long had it been since she had been away from this wreck of a farmhouse?

Randy looked at his watch. "Carly, I have to go to work."

"You . . . you . . . have a job?" Betty asked.

"At Faraday Fuel," he told her proudly. "In the warehouse."

She nodded. "Joe . . . my brother . . . he worked for Faraday . . . for a while." Betty looked down their driveway, as if she expected him soon.

That did it. I was ready to go after all.

"It . . . it was so good . . . to have visitors,"

Betty said. She smiled. Her eyes seemed to light up a bit. "So . . . good to . . . see . . . new faces. Thank you."

"If you want, we'll come back some time," I offered.

Betty's smile widened, and she patted my arm. "I'd . . . like that," she said faintly.

Randy and I held hands as we picked our way back across the field. "I'm really glad we did that, aren't you?" I asked. "It was just a little visit, really, but she wants us to come again. It really meant something . . . made a difference in her life."

Randy nodded. "She's nice, but her face . . . "

"I know. It was pretty awful at first, but I kind of got used to it, didn't you?"

"I don't—"

Just then Joe's old truck roared back up the driveway.

"Run!" I pulled Randy the rest of the way across the field and through the trees. Then I let go of his hand and ran through the stream to the other side. I didn't even care when my sneakers got soaked.

"Carly, what's wrong?" Randy was taking his time crossing on the rocks.

I dropped onto the bank and hugged my knees to stop from shaking. "I didn't want Joe to see us!"

Randy sat down beside me. "Why?"

I told him about Joe chasing Alison with the tractor.

"What!" Randy took both my hands and looked me straight in the eye. "Carly, promise me you'll never go over there again."

"But Betty'll be looking forward to a visit! You saw how excited she was to have company."

"You can't go! What if Joe caught you in his house?"

"We can watch for him to come back, like today. Randy, we have to go over there again! Betty is old and sick and . . . "

He was frowning. "But you can't make her well."

"Maybe not, but we can make her smile! Remember how she smiled at us? I bet she hasn't smiled like that for years!"

He leaned closer, so his face was just inches from mine. "Carly, listen. Don't go back there! You might get hurt! And anyway, you can't try to solve all the problems in the world. Maybe you've been spending too much time with Alison."

I jumped to my feet and glared at him. "Alison would *want* to help Betty! Maybe I've been spending too much time with *you*!"

I turned and stumbled through the trees to the park.

"Carly!" Randy called. "Wait!"

But I didn't stop when I heard him following. I ran past the swings and raced toward home, and didn't look back until I finally turned the corner by my house. The sidewalk was empty. I didn't know if I was relieved or disappointed.

When I got inside, I went upstairs, kicked off my wet sneakers, and threw myself on my bed. How could Randy turn his back on someone like Betty? How could he not care?

At the same time, I had to admit I was afraid to go back to the farmhouse by myself.

I stared at the ceiling, thinking. Randy wouldn't go again. Alison was more scared of Joe than I was. And she hadn't even seen Betty's face.

But now, after actually talking with her, how would it be possible to see Betty sitting alone on her porch swing, day after day, and not ever say another thing to her? I wanted to let her know I cared—but how?

One thing was sure. I didn't have to worry about "spending too much time" with Randy. He probably wouldn't ever call again.

I walked over to Alison's. She sat close beside me on her bed while I told her everything.

"Hmm . . . I don't know what to tell you, Carly. I mean, you've got to help other people, right? You have to do what you can. But then there's Joe." Alison shivered. "You never can tell when he'll show up, you know. Maybe Randy's right. You *should* stay away!"

"But if you had met Betty . . . " Sure, I realized. Then you'd really think I was crazy to go back. Betty's skin was a hundred times worse than a rash from poison ivy.

Suddenly I had a truly scary thought. What if Betty's blisters *weren't* some kind of family problem? What if they were contagious? Did I touch her? Did Randy?

"Carly, are you okay?" Alison leaned closer. "I mean, your face just got so white!"

I couldn't tell her what I was thinking. "I'm fine . . . just worried about Betty." And myself. And even Randy.

"Well, what I mean is," Alison continued, "I think Randy really likes you and just wants to, you know, protect you from Joe."

"Maybe." Did Betty touch me? She patted my arm! I glanced down, but all I saw were the same freckles here and there.

"So don't go to the farmhouse again, okay? Maybe you could call Betty on the phone, you know, and talk to her. But don't go over there, okay? Promise?" She reached over and gave me a hug to help me decide.

"Oh, okay," I mumbled.

Alison smiled in relief. "That's great! I mean, I'm really glad. Hey, did I tell you about the new guy I met—Dillon? He lives four houses down the street from Cecily."

While Alison talked, I checked my arm again, but it still looked okay. My shoulders relaxed a little. Maybe those blisters weren't contagious. Maybe everyone in Betty and Joe's family had this problem. But I had better be careful until I found out for sure.

When I got home, I checked our phone book. Betty and her brother weren't listed. They probably didn't even have a phone. If I wanted to talk to Betty, I'd have to go over there, even though I promised Alison I wouldn't.

And Dad would have a fit if he found out I had been there even once. I wished I hadn't told him about Joe chasing Alison with the tractor.

Being a friend to Betty was going to be a lot harder than I thought. But if my grandma back in Indianapolis were so alone and so sick, I hoped someone would come and talk to her. I just didn't know if I was brave enough to go to the farmhouse by myself.

Four

WITHOUT Jeremy around, the rest of the week dragged by. Even school would have been more exciting. I was having a hard time staying mad at Randy, and every time the phone rang, I hoped it was him. But usually it was Alison—or someone trying to sell something. I didn't go to see Betty again, but I kept trying to think of ways to talk to her.

Finally it was Monday morning. When I got to Jeremy's house, he was really glad to see me—and I was just as glad to see him. It surprised me how much I had missed the little guy.

Ginny came in from the kitchen. "Show Carly your arms, Jeremy."

He held them out. His skin was smooth and clear.

"That's great, Jeremy!" But not great for

Freckles, I added silently. He really was allergic to her.

While Ginny bustled around getting ready for work, I handed Jeremy the new plastic boat I had been holding behind my back.

Jeremy couldn't wait to try it out, so we headed for the park as soon as Ginny left. It was so hot that I splashed in the stream with him. Then he talked me into carrying buckets of water to the sandbox to make the sand nice and wet. He must have had a good time, because we did just about the same thing the next day.

Off and on, I wondered about Betty, but it wasn't until Wednesday morning that I saw her. I was filling a bucket at the stream and spotted her on her porch. I waved, but she didn't look my way. The red pickup was parked in front of the farmhouse, so I wasn't tempted to try a quick visit. Anyway, I sure couldn't take Jeremy with me.

By Thursday morning, though, I had something else to think about. I was playing with Jeremy in the sandbox when I noticed faint pink dots on the inside of his arm. I glanced at his other arm. More dots.

"What's wrong, Carly?"

I forced a smile. "Nothing, honey." I tossed my shovel in our bag of toys. "But let's go home now, okay?"

When he stood up, I saw spots behind his knees, too. What in the world could be causing the rash this time? Jeremy hadn't been around any animals that I knew of. And now his nose was running, besides. That's all he needed—a summer cold.

Ginny was already home when we got there.

"Are we late?" I asked. My watch said 11:05.

Ginny shook her head wearily. "No, I had a bad morning, that's all. I decided to come home early." She was on the couch in the family room with her feet on the coffee table and her eyes half-closed.

"Can I help?" I asked.

She smiled a little. "Well, you could buy the house at 304 Bentwood. A couple was supposed to sign the papers to buy it today, but they never showed up. I spent weeks showing them houses. I was sure they'd buy this one."

She closed her eyes.

Great, I thought. Ginny really needs more bad news.

"Come here and give me a hug, Jeremy," she called.

Uh-oh! "Um, Ginny . . . you need to check Jeremy's arms."

When she did, her shoulders sagged even more. "I'll call Dr. Graves again," she said with a sigh.

She got an appointment late that afternoon. Ginny called me shortly after they got back, just as Dad and I finished dinner.

"The doctor still says Jeremy has an allergy," she said. "He thinks it's making his nose run, too. I told him you-know-who was gone, but he says Jeremy must be allergic to other things, too. He wants him to go to an allergist to find out what they are." She sighed. "We have an appointment next Tuesday afternoon."

After I hung up and filled Dad in, he said, "Don't worry, Carly. It's probably not serious."

"I hope not."

I carried my plate to the sink and rinsed it. Then I nearly dropped it. A few spots of rash were on the inside of *my* arm. Both arms. I swallowed hard and glanced at Dad. He was drinking his coffee and watching the news on the kitchen TV.

I put my plate in the dishwasher and went up to my room. My legs felt so wobbly, it was hard to walk.

After I closed my bedroom door, I felt behind my knees. *More bumps*. I shivered involuntarily. How could this happen? How could Jeremy and I suddenly be allergic to the same thing? I never had any allergies before.

But . . . what if Jeremy's rash *wasn't* from allergies after all? What if it was contagious? Maybe I should have been worried about getting *his* rash instead of Betty's blisters!

My hand shook when I dialed Alison's number, and my voice quivered as I filled her in.

"That's awful!" she said. "You think you got it from Jeremy?" Alison's voice sounded far away. I knew she was checking her own arms and legs for spots.

"I hope this allergist can figure out what's causing his rash," I said. "Then maybe I'll know what to do about mine."

"You could go to your own doctor."

"Not without telling Dad. I'm not sure what he'd do if he found out I got this from Jeremy. He might make me stop baby-sitting. Then I'd have to spend the rest of the summer at home by myself. I'd rather have a rash."

"I'd rather stop baby-sitting," Alison admitted. "I mean, especially if your rash spreads, you know, like Jeremy's did. Are you going to tell Ginny or anything?"

I thought for a second. "I guess not. She'd feel bad that I caught it. Anyway, she has enough problems right now. Maybe I can get rid of it without her ever knowing."

Alison and I talked for a while longer, then hung up. As soon as I put the phone down, it rang again.

"Are you still mad at me?"

Randy!

"Uh, no, not that I remember."

"Then would you come to the beach with me on Saturday?"

The beach? That meant wearing a bathing suit. My rash would show. Randy knew about Jeremy's rash and might figure everything out. Did I want him to know?

"I . . . I'm not sure, Randy."

"Carly, I'm sorry for everything I said last week. I know you were just trying to help a sick old lady."

"It's not that. It's just, well, going swimming."

"Oh. Well, okay," he mumbled. "My sister . . . I know. . . . Maybe next week would be better. Bye." He hung up.

I sat on the floor with the phone in my hand. Why did he hang up so fast? And what did his sister have to do with it? *Maybe next week would be better?* What did he mean?

Then it hit me! Randy thought I was having my period! I closed my eyes and sank to the floor. Great. How could I ever look him in the eye again?

Five

MONDAY morning Jeremy and I were putting a puzzle together on the kitchen table when the doorbell rang—again and again and again.

When I opened the door, Cecily smiled sweetly up at me. Then she pushed the doorbell again.

Alison was behind her and grabbed her hand. "Cecily! You're supposed to stop when someone answers, you know!"

Cecily stomped into the house. "Jeremy! I'm heeere!"

I hoped he had time to hide.

"We gotta talk," Alison whispered as she came inside. She looked tense, which was normal for someone baby-sitting Cecily, but why was she whispering?

"Wait till you see—" Alison began.

"I know where that goes!" Cecily interrupted

from the kitchen, loud enough for the neighbors to hear. We reached the door in time to see her snatch a puzzle piece out of Jeremy's hand.

"Hey!" Jeremy grabbed it back and held it over his head.

"Cecily!" Alison called as the little girl gathered herself to lunge at Jeremy. "Come and show Carly your new dress!"

Cecily forgot about the puzzle and pranced over to us. Alison held Cecily's arms out to show me her new yellow sun dress.

Then my heart almost stopped. Alison wasn't really showing me the dress. She was holding Cecily's arms so I could see the pink rash on the inside of both elbows. I glanced at Alison and she nodded. Her eyes looked scared. Now I understood why she wanted to talk.

"That's a very pretty dress, Cecily," I managed to say. I got a box of graham crackers out of the cupboard. "Why don't you two go out in the backyard and eat some crackers, okay?"

Cecily grabbed the box. "Okay!"

"You better give me some," Jeremy muttered as he followed her out the back door.

Alison's freckles stood out on her pale face. "I just noticed those spots this morning. Carly, I'm . . . you know, I'm scared!"

I shook my head. "Jeremy must really be

contagious!" I pulled up my sleeves. My own spots had faded a little over the weekend.

"At least I don't have it yet." Alison held out her arms so I could see they were still okay.

"That's good," I said. "And Ginny must not have it either. I think she'd tell me if she did."

Wait a minute. Something was wrong here. "Alison, don't you think Ginny would catch Jeremy's rash before Cecily got it?"

She frowned. "Yeah. Ginny's around him a lot more than Cecily, right?"

"Maybe . . . maybe Jeremy's not contagious after all. Maybe he, Cecily, and I all touched the same thing. Something like poison ivy, something that gives *everyone* a rash."

Alison nodded. "Something Ginny didn't touch—or me either, I guess. But what?" Her eyes darted around the kitchen as if she expected something to jump out at her.

Just then the back door burst open. "There's nothing to do out there!" Cecily shouted. "I want to swing at the park!"

Jeremy came in behind her. "I want to sail my boat," he mumbled through a mouthful of crackers.

Cecily whirled around to face Jeremy. She put her hands on her hips. "Then you have to wait till I go home and get mine! No fair going to the park without me!"

Cecily had a boat now, too. She liked the swings better, but lately she had spent a lot of time playing in the stream.

Then it hit me. "The *stream*," I whispered to Alison. "We've all been in the stream. There must be something in the water." I could feel goose bumps popping out on my arms.

Alison's face turned white. "But I've been in the stream too."

"Not as much as the three of us."

Alison checked her arms again and hugged herself. "What could be in there?"

I shook my head. "I don't know. The water looks so clean."

"Why are you whispering?" Cecily yelled. "Are you telling secrets?"

"Ah . . . no, 'course not," Alison told her. "But, um, we can't go to the park today. It's going to rain, you know."

Cecily looked out the kitchen window. The sky was cloudless. "But . . . "

I spied Jeremy's can of clay on the counter.

"Who can make the longest snake?" I opened the can and tossed them each a big lump.

"Me!" Cecily immediately started rolling hers on the table.

"No, me!" Jeremy insisted.

Alison pulled me to the other end of the kitchen. "What if there's poison or chemicals or something in the stream?" she whispered. Her eyes widened. "I mean, what if it's got toxic waste in it!"

Cecily had stopped making her snake and was watching Alison.

"No secrets, Cecily. Everything's okay," I said, even though it wasn't. My voice was shaky and my goose bumps were back.

Cecily looked at us suspiciously. Then she started pulling her snake apart and mashing the chunks flat with her fist.

"But where would toxic waste come from?" I whispered to Alison. "The only thing around here is ordinary houses."

"What about Faraday Fuel? I bet that place is crawling with, you know, chemicals and other stuff!"

"But it's on the other side of town. It must be five miles away. How would any chemicals from Faraday get in that stream?"

"I don't know, but . . . but I still think they did." Alison started to tremble. "I mean, this makes me think about Love Canal! Remember the report I did in health?"

How could I forget? Alison had told the class how a big company had buried barrels of toxic chemicals in a place called Love Canal. Then people built houses and even a school on the land because they didn't know the chemicals were there.

After a while, people who lived in the houses started getting sick. Babies were born dead or had birth defects. It was a long time before anyone realized toxic chemicals were leaking from barrels buried under their houses.

"This can't be like Love Canal!" I was trembling now, too.

"But what if it *is*?" Alison whispered. "I mean, what if we're all being slowly poisoned or something? These houses haven't been here very long, you know, maybe seven or eight years. Who knows what's buried under them—or under the park?"

Please, I prayed, let this all just be Alison's imagination. I glanced at the kids. Jeremy was making lumpy monsters now, but Cecily was watching us and frowning.

I forced myself to smile. "What are you making, Cecily?"

She looked down at the blobs of clay she had squashed on the table. "Spots."

"Good work!"

She nodded and stole one of Jeremy's monsters while he was busy making more.

"We have to warn everyone about the stream!" Alison whispered.

"We don't even know for sure!"

"Carly, we can't wait until we all get sick or

something before we tell people what we think! I mean, shouldn't you at least tell Ginny?"

Should I? Ginny had felt so bad when she lost that sale last week. I knew she'd feel worse—much worse—if she thought the stream in her park might be full of toxic waste.

I shook my head. "I don't think I'll tell her, not until we're sure. Maybe there isn't anything to worry about. Maybe all three of us really *are* allergic to the same thing."

I didn't believe that for a minute, though.

"But what if we find out a year from now the stream really is polluted?" Alison persisted. "By then everyone might be, you know, really sick. I mean, what if that rash is the beginning of cancer or something?"

I closed my eyes. Maybe I *should* tell Ginny.

Then I had a better idea. "I know what we can do! We'll just stay away from the stream. Remember how Jeremy's rash disappeared when he went to his grandparents? It wasn't because he was away from Freckles. He was away from the stream!"

"But—"

"Alison, if we all stay out of the water, this rash will go away and never come back. Then we won't have to say anything to anyone!"

"Yeah, but what about the other kids, Carly? Last week I saw two little boys building a dam across the stream."

Alison was right. As the neighbor kids found out the stream was there, more and more of them would go to play in the water. Suddenly I felt too tired to stand up.

"I'm done!" Jeremy slipped off his chair and ran into the family room. A second later we could hear cartoon voices.

"I mean, we have to let everyone know," Alison whispered to me. "Let's call the Seaside Sentinel and tell them what Faraday is doing!"

"But we don't know Faraday is doing anything! And if we call the newspaper, they'll put our names in the story. The people at Faraday will read it, for sure. And if we're wrong, they'll fire my dad for having such a trouble-maker for a daughter! Then he'll have to find another job. We'll probably have to move again!"

Alison put her arm around me. "Carly, you know I don't want that to happen, but we have to do something!"

Just then Ginny's car pulled in the driveway. Alison and I eyed each other nervously.

"Let's think about it some more, okay?" I said. "We have to be sure before we tell anyone."

"Okay, but we can't keep quiet for long, you know. I'll come over to your house this afternoon, as soon as Cecily's mom gets home. We have to decide what to do!"

Six

ABOUT an hour later, I was in our kitchen finishing off a peanut butter sandwich when Alison burst in the front door.

"Carly, where are you? I know what we should do!"

"Back here!" I called. "Tell me!"

She hurried back and headed straight for our phone. "We'll call the city and, you know, ask them to check the stream. They can tell if there are chemicals or something in it!"

"They can tell everyone we called, too."

"Not if we don't tell them our names," she said. "I mean, it's not like they'll recognize our voices or something."

"Maybe they can trace the call."

"Nah! This isn't a spy movie, you know! This is real life!"

I shook my head. "It doesn't seem real today."

But Alison had already flipped the phone book open to "Seaside, city of." She ran her finger down a column of numbers.

"How about the Parks and Recreation Department? I mean, the stream's in a park and all, right?" Alison pushed the phone toward me and smiled. "Here's the number, Carly."

I sighed and dialed the one she was pointing to.

A woman answered. "Seaside Parks and Rec. Can I help you?"

"Um," I mumbled, "my friend and I, we're kind of worried about a stream that's in a park and, uh, we wonder if . . . if you would come and check the water?"

"Honey, we don't do that here. Why don't you try the Seaside Water Treatment Plant— or maybe the County Board of Health?"

A man at the Water Treatment Plant told me to call the State Board of Health or the State Department of Natural Resources. Those were both long distance numbers, so I tried the County Board of Health. It even had a number for "environmental health."

The phone rang about twelve times. A woman finally answered with a quick "Yes?"

"Is this . . . uh . . . environmental health?"

"Of course. What's your problem?"

She wasn't making this any easier. "Uh, we're worried about the water in a stream and—"

"What township?"

"Township?" I couldn't remember.

"Madison," Alison whispered.

"Madison," I told the woman.

"Well, then," she said, "give me your name and phone number."

"Why?"

She didn't answer at first. "The person responsible for your township—and several other townships, I might add—is out of the office. He'll have to call you back when he has time."

"Well, could I just call again later?"

"Young lady, why don't you just tell me your name and phone number? You could save us both a lot of time that way."

I didn't know what to say.

"Young lady?"

"Uh, I'd rather not tell you."

"Well, in that case, whatever you wanted can't be very important. Please stop bothering busy people."

I looked at Alison. "She hung up!"

Alison stuck her tongue out at the phone. "I bet she wouldn't do that to an adult. I wish we could get someone older to call for us.

Then we'd get some action!"

"But who?" I asked. "How about your mom or dad?"

Alison rolled her eyes. "They probably wouldn't believe the stream needs to be checked or anything. I mean, last week Mom told me I was always worried about something. As if I should just forget about the poor dolphins, right?"

Alison had asked her mom to stop buying a certain brand of tuna fish because tuna nets trapped dolphins, too, and they drowned. I didn't want dolphins to drown either, but I could see how her parents might get a little impatient sometimes. Still, the stream was different. Maybe everyone in Seaside should be worried about it.

"What about your dad?" Alison asked. "We could tell him we think something's in the stream without, you know, ever mentioning Faraday. Then he could call someone to come and check the water. I mean, he wouldn't get in trouble at work for just being a good citizen, right?"

That sounded like a good plan to me, so that night after dinner I brought it up. I waited until Dad poured his second cup of coffee.

"So, how are things going at work?" I asked.

Dad was the manager of the Human Resources Department at Faraday. That meant he hired and fired people.

"Busy, really busy. We've got a big government report due on Friday. If we miss the deadline, it'll cost Faraday a lot of money." He smiled as he stirred his coffee. "But I've got a good group of people in my department. We'll get it done on time."

Sometimes it was scary how much Dad liked his job.

He turned on the TV sitting on the kitchen counter. The evening news was starting.

"Uh, Dad? Remember that rash Jeremy has?"

"Uh-huh." Dad reached over and changed the channel.

"At first Jeremy's doctor thought he was allergic to Freckles, remember? But his rash came back after Ginny gave Freckles away."

Dad looked at me and nodded. Then he went back to the TV.

"Well, Jeremy plays in the stream a lot. You know—the one I told you about at the new park?"

Dad nodded again, but he didn't take his eyes off the TV.

"So Alison and I think . . . we think maybe . . . um . . . something's in the water."

"Oh?" A man on TV was talking about the stock market. Dad took a little notebook out of his shirt pocket and wrote some numbers on it.

"Dad, we think the stream's polluted."

He stopped writing and looked at me. "Polluted? With what?"

"Something that causes a rash, maybe some kind of . . . of chemical." I was getting awfully close to blaming Faraday.

Dad's eyebrows shot up. "What kind of chemical?"

"Well, I don't know, really." I didn't sound too convincing, even to myself.

"Whose idea was this, Carly?"

"Well, first I thought there might be something in the water, and then Alison—"

"—decided it was a chemical, right? A toxic chemical?"

I nodded. How did Dad know that?

"Carly, I like Alison, but . . . " He shook his head. "Is she still boycotting tuna fish?"

I knew I shouldn't have told him about that.

"Dad, this really *is* a problem! I'm worried, too. Something keeps giving Jeremy a rash and it's not Freckles."

Should I tell him I had a rash, too? And Cecily? Or would he think we caught it from

Jeremy? Would he make me stop baby-sitting?

Dad patted my hand. "Honey, I'm sure Jeremy's mom will figure out what's bothering him. You don't need to worry about it. In the meantime, why don't you try to find some more friends? How about calling that girl who asked you to her birthday party just before school was out? What was her name? Susan?"

I shook my head. "Dad, I don't need more friends—"

"What about that boy you went to the movies with? Ralph?"

"Randy."

He nodded. "I liked him. Maybe we could go to the beach Saturday and you could invite him, okay?"

Oh, sure, I thought. After he asked me last week and I . . . no way.

"Maybe," I mumbled.

For sure, Dad wasn't going to call and get the stream checked. In fact, if I wasn't careful, he might want me to stop being friends with Alison. I put the dishes in the dishwasher and headed upstairs to call her.

Alison listened carefully, then said, "Carly, maybe I should talk to your dad," she said. "You know, sort of explain about toxic waste and things."

"Uh . . . I don't think so. When he makes

his mind up, that's it." I hadn't told her *everything* Dad said.

"Darn! Who else . . . wait, I've got it! Randy works in the warehouse—that's probably where they keep all those chemicals and everything! Why don't you call and invite him to the beach, you know, like your dad wanted you to. While you're talking, ask him to kind of check around and find out if Faraday is dumping chemicals."

"The beach? But—"

"Hey, you've *got* to talk to him again sometime! Anyway, so what if he knows girls have periods? I mean, it just proves he paid attention in health!"

After we hung up, I started to dial Randy's number about four times and hung up each time. Finally, I did it.

"Hello?"

"Uh, Randy? It's me, Carly. Um . . . would you like to go to the beach this weekend?"

"Are *you* going to be there?"

"What? Sure . . . Dad and I—"

"Well, then, okay! I just didn't want to be there all by myself."

"Randy . . . " I heard him chuckle.

Remember the real reason you called, I told myself. "So, how's your job going? Do you still work in the warehouse?"

"Yup! I'm even learning how to drive the forklift."

"Do you ever move . . . chemicals?"

"Not me. Only the older guys move those. Why?"

I took a big breath. "Remember Jeremy's rash?"

"I guess so. What about it?"

"Um, maybe those chemicals are causing it."

"Carly, I bet Jeremy has never even been near the warehouse."

"Maybe the chemicals came to him."

"I don't think Faraday has delivered any chemicals to Jeremy's house, either."

"Maybe they came in the stream. You know, the one in the park? It might have chemicals in it and—"

"From Faraday? Not a chance!"

"But how can you be sure? Maybe . . . maybe some chemicals were accidentally dumped in the stream."

"Carly, you should see all the government forms my boss has to fill out to keep track of toxic stuff. Faraday has to know where it is every second. There's no way any of it could 'accidentally' end up in any stream."

He almost had me convinced—until I thought of something. "The warehouse stores new chemicals, right? But after Faraday uses them, there must be some stuff left over, like chemical garbage? That kind of stuff doesn't come back to the warehouse, does it?"

"No, but—"

"Well, maybe Faraday isn't so careful with leftover chemicals. Maybe they *are* just dumped someplace."

"Nah."

"But could you just check around and find out what happens to them?"

"Carly, you need a special badge to go into the areas where they use those chemicals, and I don't have one. If someone catches me where I'm not supposed to be, I might get fired!"

"Maybe if you explained—"

"What could I say? I have to check things out because Carly Hendricks is worried about a stream?"

"Not just me! Alison—"

"I should have guessed."

"Randy, I know Alison gets carried away sometimes, but this is different. Honest!"

"This is different, all right—this is serious stuff! If you and Alison go around saying Faraday put chemicals in that stream, someone might believe you. They might call the media. Then reporters would bring TV cameras and—"

"But—"

"—and the people at Faraday would be really mad. First they'd prove you're wrong. Then I bet they'd sue you for thousands of dollars, just for making them look bad."

"Sue me?" Randy had to be making that up.

"Well, maybe they can't sue you because you're not old enough. Maybe they'd sue your dad instead."

Right after they fired him, I told myself. The cold lump was back in my stomach.

"But what if Alison and I are right? What then? Should we just be quiet so no one will get mad—and Faraday can keep dumping chemicals?"

"Faraday isn't dumping chemicals."

"How do you *know*?" It was time to tell him everything. "Randy, something in that stream *does* cause a rash. I have one now, too. So does the little girl Alison baby-sits."

"You have a rash?"

"Just like Jeremy's. I got it after I went in the stream and carried buckets of that water to the sandbox. It splashed all over me." I just remembered that. I glanced down at my arms. The spots were fading, thank goodness.

For a minute Randy was quiet. "But even if there *are* chemicals in the stream, it doesn't mean they're from Faraday. They could be from a gas station . . . some place like that.

Sometimes those underground gasoline tanks leak."

"Maybe," I said skeptically. "But we have to find out for sure. Then we can call the police or someone. They'll stop *whoever's* doing this. If we don't do anything, a lot of little kids will get sick from that stream. They might . . . they might even get cancer. Doesn't that scare you a little?"

"Well, sure, but—"

"Then look around at Faraday," I begged. "Find out what happens to the leftover chemicals."

"I don't think I can."

"You just don't want to!" I hung up.

Why did I ever think I liked Randy? First he didn't want me to visit Betty and now he wouldn't help stop little kids from getting sick. What *did* he care about, anyway?

But, I reminded myself, you and Alison might be wrong about the stream. Tomorrow, Jeremy's allergist might find some simple reason for that rash. Maybe some day you'll laugh about this.

I doubted it, though. And meanwhile, all I could do was wait—and hope Jeremy's allergy doctor ran tests that showed something, something not too scary, something that would explain all this.

Seven

ON Tuesday morning Jeremy wanted to go to the park, but I talked him into making cookies instead. After Ginny got home, they left for the allergist. I went back to my house and took a blanket and a new book into the backyard to kill time until they got back.

I must have dozed off in the sun. Suddenly a deep voice yelled, "There you are! No wonder you didn't answer the doorbell!"

I sat up. Randy was walking around the corner of our house. He held up his hands. "Before you say anything, I'm sorry about yesterday." He dropped down on the blanket beside me. "I thought a lot about that stream last night. So today, I asked my boss what Faraday does with used chemicals."

"You did? What did he say?"

"You were right about one thing, Carly.

Faraday does have lots of chemicals and other dangerous stuff left over after the fuel is processed."

"I thought so."

"But," he said with a smile, "they're really careful with it. My boss says Faraday is so good at handling toxic waste that other companies come here to learn how they do it."

"So how *do* they do it?" Randy seemed convinced, but I wasn't.

"Well . . . " He crossed his legs. "Some chemicals dissolve easily in water. Faraday mixes those with solid material and then forms the material into bricks. Then they put a waterproof coating on the bricks to trap the chemicals inside. And then they put the bricks in a special landfill lined with packed clay and sheets of plastic. After all that, the chemicals can't possibly leak into any streams."

He grinned and reached for my hand. "See? Faraday really is careful. And I really do care about little kids, Carly."

Randy was so close that I was having trouble thinking. "Okay, so . . . is that the only way Faraday gets rid of used chemicals?"

"Nope. Sometimes they mix dangerous chemicals with chemicals that make them safe. One chemical cancels the other one out, like mixing acids with bases, you know?"

"Hmm. I think I heard about that in science class."

"And Faraday recycles some chemicals, like mercury and lead. They separate them out of mixtures and use them again. That even saves the company money."

He took my other hand. "Don't you see, Carly? A company that goes to all that trouble isn't going to turn around and dump chemicals in a stream, right?"

Randy sat there smiling, waiting for me to agree. I could feel the tightness melt out of my shoulders. Those chemicals couldn't be coming from Faraday. We didn't have to accuse them of anything. And Faraday wouldn't fire Dad—or sue us.

I squeezed Randy's hand a little. "Thanks for finding out."

"That's okay. My boss was impressed that I wanted to know." He chuckled. "I didn't tell him it was your idea." He leaned toward me and tilted his head—

And the phone started ringing!

I jumped up. "It must be Ginny!"

"Wait, Carly!"

I was halfway to the house before I realized what I had just done. If I had held still, Randy would have kissed me!

"I'll be right back!" I called over my shoulder.

This better not be someone selling insurance, not after what I just passed up!

It was Ginny. "We waited forever at the allergist, and after all that, the doctor couldn't tell what's causing the rash. She said she'd have to do some tests."

"So did you tell her to go ahead with them?" I crossed my fingers, hoping that she had.

"No," said Ginny. "Jeremy's rash is fading again and his nose isn't running anymore. And those tests are so expensive. I think he'll be okay without them."

I was sure he would—if I kept him out of that stream. But what about the rest of the kids in Seaside?

I went back outside to tell Randy, but the only thing on my blanket was my book. He'd left. Did he think I didn't want to kiss him? Should I call him? What would I say?

Just then Dad came home, carrying hamburgers for dinner. After we ate, I hurried over to Alison's. She was in the kitchen, washing the dishes. I told her about Jeremy's test— and Randy. Tonight Alison was more interested in what Randy said than what he almost did.

"Well, I still think there's something bad in that water, even if Faraday didn't put it there." She rinsed off a pot. "I mean, do people have to get really sick or something before anyone will believe us?"

"I sure hope not." But as Alison stood there up to her elbows in the soapy water, I started to wonder about something else. "You know, that water doesn't seem to give anyone a rash."

Alison glanced down at her wet arms. "You're right." But she quickly checked inside her elbows, just in case.

"If the water in the stream is polluted, why isn't this water?" I wondered out loud.

Alison looked at me for a second. Then she turned toward the family room and yelled, "Mom, where does our water come from? A well or something?"

"No, it comes from a reservoir on the other side of Seaside," her mother answered. "You're probably thinking of the well we had where we lived before. That was an old house. New houses like these usually get city water."

Alison turned back to me. "I guess that explains—"

"Why do you want to know, Alison?" her mother called. "You're not worried about our water now, are you?"

Alison rolled her eyes. "No, Mom." She whispered to me, "Mom gets carried away sometimes."

I tried not to smile.

"Anyway," Alison told me, "at least now we know why this water's not polluted or anything. I bet if it came from some place close, it might have the same stuff in it as the stream."

I nodded. "I wonder if anyone around here has a well."

"Hmm . . . the only old house I can think of is Joe and Betty's. Do you think they have a well?"

"Maybe, and you can see their farmhouse from the stream, so their well would be really close to that polluted water."

A chill went up my back. Maybe Betty's blisters started as a rash, a rash just like Jeremy's, just like mine.

"I think I know what's wrong with Betty." My voice cracked. "I think there's something in their water at the farmhouse. It's the same stuff that's in the stream."

Alison's eyes got big and round. She quickly wiped her hands on a towel. "Let's go up to my room."

I was trembling by the time we got there. We sat close together on her bed.

"Betty must wash in that water." I swallowed hard. "That's why she has all those sores and blisters. The stream was doing the same thing to our skin. If we kept playing in that water, we'd all have blisters like Betty!"

Alison was rubbing her arms. Her freckles stood out on her pale face. "Now we *really* have to warn everyone!"

I shook my head. "I bet they still wouldn't believe us. Even Betty and Joe must not realize what's wrong."

We sat in silence for a minute. Then a ray of sun broke through my gloom. "Maybe Betty and Joe will get better if they get away from that water!" I said. "Maybe it's not too late! We have to help them!"

"But how? I mean, we can't go over there and drag them out of their house."

"I know. And even if we could get them out, that stuff would still be in the stream. And kids would still play in it."

"Maybe we could, you know, put up our own signs and warn everyone to stay out of the water."

I could imagine what my dad and Alison's parents would say if we did that. But we had to do something. I had one more idea.

"What if we follow the stream and see if we can find out what's leaking into it?"

Alison frowned. "Us?"

"Sure. That stuff has to be coming from someplace. Maybe we can find it. Then people would have to believe us and clean it up." I remembered what Randy had said: "Maybe the stream goes past an old gas station or some other place that has chemicals and toxic stuff."

Alison thought for a minute and smiled. "If we could find the place—and not get too close, you know—we'd be heroes! I mean, maybe they'd put our pictures in the paper: 'Teenagers Save Seaside from Toxic Pollution!'"

"Maybe." That sounded kind of embarrassing to me, but at least it was an incentive for Alison to come with me. "The pollution must be upstream. If we follow the water we'll find it."

Alison's frown slipped back over her face. "But the stream is on the edge of Joe's field. I mean, what if it goes, you know, right across his land? We can't follow it there!"

"If it goes there, we'll be careful. He won't even see us."

"But what if he does? I mean, what would he do if he caught us sneaking around?" She was as pale as ever. "Carly, I'm worried about the stream and everything, but we can't go on Joe's land. Even with two of us, it's too scary!"

"What if . . . what if Randy came with us? Would you go then?"

"Well . . . he's a pretty big guy and everything, maybe bigger than Joe. I mean, Joe might think twice before he messed with

Randy." She nodded a little. "I guess . . . I guess I'd go if Randy came, too. I mean, we've got to do something, right?"

"Right! I'll call Randy tonight and ask him. Let's check out the stream tomorrow, after I'm done baby-sitting. I'll meet you and Randy at the park about 12:30, okay?"

Alison sighed and hugged herself. "I'm still not sure about this, Carly. I mean, I really want to help, you know, but Joe. . . ."

I gave Alison's arm a squeeze. "Maybe Randy and I could just walk a little bit up the stream and see what's there. Then we'll come back and tell you."

She hesitated a minute and shook her head. "No. You and me are in this together. I mean, if you're brave enough to go, I guess I am, too." She smiled a little. "I'll be at the park at 12:30, in my grungiest jeans and everything."

I hurried home and called Randy.

"Want to go hiking?" I asked.

"Hiking? Where? This doesn't have anything to do with that stream, does it?"

"Well, actually . . . " How did he guess?

"Carly, there's nothing in that stream! I told you Faraday—"

"And I believe you, but remember Betty's skin?"

"How could I forget?"

"Well, now I think I know what's wrong with her." Don't mention Alison, I told myself. "I'm almost sure the water at her house is polluted with the same stuff as the stream. I bet Betty's been around that water so long her rash has turned into blisters."

At first Randy didn't say anything. "Carly, even if you're right, she doesn't just have blisters. She's really sick. Remember how much trouble she had breathing? And that oxygen tank she has to use?"

The hair on the back of my neck stood up. "Whatever's in the water must hurt your breathing, too. Jeremy's nose used to run after he'd been in the stream. We thought he had a cold. And his eyes would get red and watery, like Betty's." I swallowed, but the lump in my throat stayed where it was. "It was all caused by that polluted water—I just know it."

Randy sighed. "But if you believe me about Faraday, who or what do you think is polluting the water?"

"I don't know. That's why we're going to follow the stream and see if we can find out."

"We? You and me?"

I bit my lip. "Well, Alison wants to come, too, but she's worried that we might end up on Joe's land. We're hoping you'll come and

79

scare away any bad guys who show up."

"I doubt Joe would be scared of me."

"Alison and I would still feel a lot safer if you came."

"You'd be a lot safer if you stayed home. When were you going to do this, anyway?"

"Tomorrow afternoon," I told him, "after I baby-sit Jeremy."

"I have to work in the afternoon."

I had forgotten about his job! "Could you take a day off?"

"They need me and, besides, I don't even want you to follow that stream. I think it does cross Joe's farm. From what you told me, I also think he's a little crazy. If he catches you—"

"But no one believes there's anything dangerous in that water. This is our chance to prove it! If we could find something leaking—"

"What if Joe finds you first?"

"He won't! Come on, Randy! Meet us at the park at 12:30, okay?"

"I *can't*. I have to be at work by noon. Carly, please don't do this."

"Just go to work, Randy. We'll be fine without you."

I hung up and flopped onto my bed. Randy! He said he cared about little kids, but when he had a chance to prove it, he couldn't take a little time off his job!

And now I had another problem. Should I call Alison and tell her Randy probably wasn't coming? Maybe she wouldn't go then. And we had to. Every day Betty was probably getting a little sicker. And every day more kids would find that stream and splash polluted water all over themselves.

I wondered if Alison would come without Randy. No one cared more than she did about stopping pollution and protecting little kids. Still, I figured it might be better if I didn't tell her about Randy until the last minute. Maybe then she'd come anyway.

I sure hoped so. I didn't know if I were brave enough to go alone. The stream probably did cross Joe's land.

Eight

I watched the stream ripple over the stones in its path as I waited for Alison. The water was as clear—and lifeless—as ever. At least now I understood why nothing swam there.

And that faint smell was still in the air. I had smelled it somewhere else, too, but where? Then I remembered—at the old farmhouse. A shiver raced along my skin.

I checked my watch. 12:42. Alison should have been here by now. And Randy, if he changed his mind.

A few minutes later, I heard a commotion in the trees. My heart did a little leap. Was that him?

But it was only two boys pushing through the trees. They were eight or nine years old and wearing only shorts and sneakers. The blond one carried a plastic bucket, and his dark-haired friend had a small fish net.

"What are you doing here?" I asked, as if it were my business.

They backed away a little. The blond nodded at the stream. "We're going to catch some stuff."

You'll catch some stuff, I thought, but not what you expect.

"Well, the stream's closed today." I stood up straighter and tried to look as if I were in charge. Maybe they wouldn't notice my torn jeans and backpack.

The dark-haired boy glanced around. "Why? There's no sign that says it's closed."

"I'm waiting for someone to bring it now," I lied. "You'll have to play somewhere else."

The blond hesitated. Then he said, "C'mon, Michael," and they headed back through the trees.

At least I knew they hadn't spent much time here, not if they expected to find any-thing alive in this water.

"Where's your sign?" I heard one of the boys say to someone.

"Sign? What sign?" It was Alison! She had come after all!

She was shaking her head as she pushed through the greenery. "Carly, did you ever notice how, you know, strange the kids are around here?"

I smiled. "They're weird all right. Ready to go?"

"I guess, as soon as Randy gets here."

Uh-oh. I glanced at my watch. Nearly one o'clock. He wasn't coming. "Uh, I forgot about Randy's job, Alison. He has to work this afternoon."

Alison just looked at me a second. Then she slumped against a tree and started chewing her lip.

"We won't go very far upstream, okay?" I said. "And we'll come back whenever you want to, okay?"

"Promise? I mean, really and truly promise?"

I swallowed. "I promise. I'm a little scared, too, but we have to do this, Alison. We have to. Do you smell something?"

She sniffed the air. "Yeah. I smelled it here before." She rubbed her nose with her hand.

"It was a lot worse at Betty's house. It's the chemicals or whatever is polluting the water."

Alison glanced at the stream and quickly stepped back.

"And you know those two boys you just saw?" I asked.

"You mean the strange ones?"

I smiled a little. "They weren't strange. They just wanted to play in the stream. I told them a story so they'd go away, but I bet they come back as soon as we leave."

Alison frowned at the trickling water. Then

she nodded. "I know what you're saying. I mean, we've got to do this, no matter what. Let's go."

I went first, heading upstream with Alison behind me.

The trees and bushes crowded close to the stream in places. "Watch out here," I said over my shoulder.

"Don't worry! I mean, the last thing I'm going to do is step in that water."

As we got further from the park, the stream cut through woods so thick they blocked out the sun.

"I wish I had my jacket or something," Alison said. "What's in your backpack?"

"No jackets. Just a couple of cans of soda, in case we get thirsty—and an empty mayonnaise jar with a lid, in case we want to take something back."

"Like proof of what we find, right? Well, I don't see any, you know, leaky gas stations in the middle of these woods. Ouch!" Alison had tripped over a tree root. "But at least Joe can't see us here, right?"

"Right." So far, so good.

Minutes later, though, the stream left the shelter of the trees. Up ahead, it zigzagged across a wide, abandoned cornfield. There was nothing but dried-out stubble left. A few spindly trees marked the water's path across the open field. The stream seemed to head toward another patch of woods on the far side.

I stopped at the edge of the field and Alison moved up beside me. Way over to our left, beyond the cornfield, workers were building two houses side by side.

"There's Joe's place." Alison pointed across the stream to our right. The farmhouse looked tiny, dwarfed by acres of weedy fields. "Do you think he'll see us or anything if we walk across this field?" Her voice was a little shaky.

I shook my head. "Nah. We're too far away. C'mon." I started following the stream across the field, walking fast. I held my breath until I heard her hurrying behind me.

"That smell!" Alison was panting, but she didn't ask me to slow down. "I mean, don't you think the stream stinks more now? Maybe there's more of that stuff in the water here."

"Maybe." Were we getting close to whatever was polluting the stream? I couldn't see anything ahead but more trees. And a low, swampy spot beside the stream. "Watch out for this mud—"

"Aeeiii!" Alison yelled.

I turned in time to see her feet slide into the stream.

"Carly, the water! The water! It's on me!"

She scrambled out of the stream and stood on the bank, staring at her legs. Her jeans were soaked to her knees, and her sneakers were brown with mud and muck.

Alison kicked off her sneakers and started unzipping her jeans. "I gotta get these off!"

"Not here!" We were in plain sight of the men building the houses.

"Carly, I'd rather walk back naked than get blisters or something!"

"You won't get blisters. You probably won't even get a rash." I hoped that was true, but the chemicals might be much stronger here. "Anyway, pretty soon we'll go back home and you can change."

"Let's go back now! You promised."

"I know, but . . . but we didn't find anything yet. How about this—I'll trade jeans and sneakers with you. Would you keep going then?"

"Trade? I mean, you'd do that, Carly?"

I was already having second thoughts, but it was too late.

"Sure. I already had that rash anyway. It wasn't so bad." I crouched behind some bushes and started to unzip my own jeans.

Alison just stood there and looked at me. "I mean, if you're that sure, I guess . . . well, we don't have to trade or anything. I guess I'll be okay. Your rash *did* go away pretty quick and everything." She frowned as she zipped her jeans up, pushed her feet into her shoes, and gingerly retied her muddy shoelaces.

I zipped my jeans and gave her a quick hug. "We won't go much farther, Alison. Honest!"

Then we hurried along the stream toward the trees on the far side of the field. Alison's sneakers squished with every step.

Finally we ducked under the tall pines. I felt even safer when the stream curved to the right, and the scrubby bushes hid us from anyone walking in the cornfield.

About five minutes later, Alison pulled on my arm. "Carly, isn't this far enough?" She was panting. "There's nothing here but trees."

"But my nose is running now." I sniffed to prove it. "We must be getting closer."

Suddenly Alison's eyes opened wide. Her fingers bit into my arm. "Carly! I hear something!" she whispered. "Someone's following us!"

We both froze. I could hear rustling behind us. Someone *was* coming!

Alison pulled me behind the nearest bushes. We crouched down, hugging each other. I could smell the muck on her sneakers.

"At least whoever's coming isn't driving a tractor," I whispered.

She nodded, but her face was chalky. We should have waited until Randy could come, I told myself. No one else knew we were here. If something happened . . .

The noise was getting closer—but after a bit I realized it was a small, rustling sound, not a man's heavy footsteps. Was it an animal? Were there bears in these woods?

I let go of Alison and tried to peek over the top of the bush. She grabbed my arm and yanked me back down, shaking her head fiercely.

"It's okay!" I whispered. "I think it's an animal."

"Oh." She looked at me with hope in her eyes. I could tell she was thinking of a fluffy bunny, not a drooling bear.

I started to rise again. Alison kept a death grip on my hand, but she didn't pull me down this time. I peeked over the bush just as a deer stopped a few yards away and sniffed the air.

I grinned down at Alison. "It's only a deer!"

"A deer?" She stood up, and we watched it turn and disappear into the trees.

"I mean, I was so scared." Alison held out her hand. It was still shaking.

"Me, too." My legs felt so wobbly I wasn't sure I could walk.

"Are you thirsty?" I reached over my shoulder

and pulled out the cans of soda.

Alison shook her head. "Let's just, you know, find whatever we're looking for and get out of here!"

I started to return the cans to my backpack, then thought better of it and put them under a tree instead. I didn't need to be toting around that extra weight, and we could always drink the sodas on our way back. Then we headed upstream again, picking our way over the uneven ground. I wiped my nose and eyes on the sleeve of my T-shirt, but they kept running.

Alison coughed behind me. "It hurts to breathe."

My throat was burning, too, but as I looked ahead, wondering how much farther we had to go, I saw the stream trickling out of a small tunnel near the bottom of a hill. Was this the end?

Alison leaned against me and put her head on my shoulder. "There's nothing here, you know, no leaky gas stations, nothing. Let's go back now, okay? I mean, I think I'm going to barf or something."

I couldn't go back now. There had to be something here. We just hadn't found it yet.

I pulled Alison over to a tree a few feet away from the water. "Sit here a minute, okay? The air's probably better here. I just want to see what's on the other side of that hill."

Alison dropped down on the pine needles. "You better stay where I can see you, Carly. And you better be careful." She pulled her knees up and leaned her forehead against them, even though her jeans were still damp.

I had to hurry. She really was getting sick.

It wasn't easy climbing the hill. And even though it made my throat burn worse, I couldn't seem to stop panting. I felt as if I had gained at least a hundred pounds in the last fifteen minutes.

I crawled the last few feet. When I got high enough to see over the top, I dropped flat on my stomach.

For a second, I forgot how much it hurt to breathe. On the other side of the hill lay a deep ravine. A huge mound of stuff had been dumped at the far end, right on top of the stream. I could see rotting cardboard boxes, mud-splattered milk cartons, shiny bits of aluminum foil, crushed cereal boxes, beer cans, and yellow newspapers.

The water flowed from under the trash heap and into the tunnel in the hill beneath me. I figured the tunnel must go all the way through the hill.

I looked harder at the stuff below. In the

middle of the trash, I saw some rusty patches. I wiped my eyes with my shirt. At least two rusty metal barrels were partly covered by the garbage. How did they get in there with the milk cartons and the cereal boxes?

And the really important question—were they leaking? Had I finally found what we'd been looking for? Were other things in that pile leaking, too—right into the stream?

"I'll be right back, Alison," I called over my shoulder.

"Carly, wait!" She coughed. "Where are you going?"

"I have to check something. Stay there."

I edged sideways a few feet so I wasn't directly over the stream. Then I pulled my legs up to the rim of the ravine and slid feet-first down the loose dirt on the other side.

By now, the air was burning a path to my lungs. I pulled the neck of my T-shirt up over my mouth, but it only helped a little.

It's down here, I told myself. Whatever's polluting the stream is down here, maybe in those barrels. You can't give up now, Carly. Get some proof. Get some proof and get out— quick.

The closer barrel was lodged high in the mound, surrounded by a jumble of moldy cardboard boxes and other stuff. I'd have to climb onto the trash to reach it.

No way, I told myself. If I slipped . . .

Then I noticed a small metal tank half-buried in dried mud at the edge of the mound. It looked a lot like Betty's oxygen tank, but I was almost sure it never held oxygen. The ground around it was a reddish-brown. The stain reached clear into the stream.

The tank had definitely leaked right into the water! Maybe it was still leaking!

My lungs were fighting for air, but every breath felt like fire.

Get proof!

Maybe I could scoop some of that red dirt into the mayonnaise jar. I hurried to the edge of the stain and knelt down, but suddenly I felt as if someone had stuffed a burning blanket in my mouth. Choking, I crawled back to the ravine wall as fast as I could.

While I tried to catch my breath, I noticed printing on the side of the little tank. Mud had splattered over some of the letters, but I could see part of the word. I wiped my eyes with my shirt again. It said "FAR . . . "

That's all I could see. It didn't matter. That was enough.

Faraday had almost fooled everyone.

Nine

GET some of that dirt, I told myself. No matter what it takes! No one will ever believe it's here if you don't take some back.

I pulled the jar out of my backpack and crawled back toward the stain, holding my breath. Keeping as far away as possible, I reached out and scooped some of the red dirt into the jar. Then I jammed on the lid, trying not to touch any dirt. It had to be full of chemicals. Instant blisters.

My lungs felt as if they were going to burst as I scrambled back to the ravine wall. They'd feel even worse, I knew, if I breathed near that tank.

I collapsed against the ravine wall and took a few shallow breaths. It felt as if I were sucking air out of a furnace. I had to get out of the ravine. I screwed the lid tightly on the jar, put it in my backpack, and zipped the top closed.

Then I glanced up the steep dirt wall, and the truth hit me. I couldn't climb back up. I was so dizzy I wasn't even sure I could stand. How long could I last in this poisoned air?

My nose began running harder. I wiped it with my hand, but my fingers came away smeared bright red! My nose was bleeding! I tipped my head back and pinched my nose shut.

Don't panic, I told myself. Just don't panic. There must be some way out of this.

"Carly?" Alison's face appeared over the edge. Her eyes were bloodshot and her face was actually dripping sweat, but I had never been so glad to see her.

"Thank God," I whispered. My voice was nearly gone.

"What happened?" Her red-rimmed eyes grew bigger. "All that blood!"

"Just my nose."

"Gross!" She coughed. "Grab on. Hurry!" She hung over the edge, reaching down with both hands.

I let go of my nose. Then I wiped my hand on my jeans, put one foot on a rock jutting out of the wall, and managed to grab one of Alison's hands. But as I pulled, she started slipping toward me, over the edge.

"Carly!" she screamed.

I let go. She scrambled away from the edge and disappeared.

"Alison?" I called hoarsely. Did she go for help? I was getting dizzier by the minute. I wouldn't be able to wait long.

Then I heard her cough. She was a little farther down the rim of the ravine. She leaned over the edge again. "Over here!"

This time she reached down with one hand. Her other arm was hooked around a sapling growing near the edge.

I shook my head to clear it and stumbled over. I climbed far enough up to grab her hand again. She pulled and I scrambled up the loose dirt as best I could. Neither of us said a word. It was hard enough just to breathe. Finally, I made it high enough to grab the sapling. Alison caught hold of my leg and pulled me over the edge.

Then we half-crawled, half-slid down the other side of the hill. For a while we just lay at the bottom, gasping. After the ravine, this air seemed almost pure.

Alison crawled closer and hugged me. "I thought you were going to die." Tears were making clean streaks down her dirty face.

"Me too. You saved me!"

"I know . . . but I'm, you know, way too tired to save you again, so can we go back now, please?" Alison asked.

I smiled a little and nodded. When we got farther away from the ravine, I would tell her what I'd found.

Alison struggled to her feet. Then she pulled me up, and we headed back downstream. She kept her arm around my waist. Twice my rubbery legs folded up, and she had to keep me from falling. When we came to the soda I'd left under the tree, we collapsed beside it without a word.

We opened the cans and took long drinks.

I sighed. Then I tipped my head back. "Did my nose stop bleeding yet?"

"Yeah, but all that blood on your shirt . . . " Alison grinned. "I mean, you look like you just had a date with Freddie Krueger."

"I kind of feel like it, too."

She nodded. "This has been awful scary. I mean, I nearly had to walk back through that cornfield all by myself." We smiled at each other. I knew she wouldn't have left me.

"And I bet we both wrecked our lungs and everything." Alison rubbed her chest and frowned. Then she looked down at her damp jeans. "No telling what's happening to my skin under there, you know."

"No telling," I admitted.

"All for . . . nothing."

"That's what you think." I fumbled with my backpack and pulled out the jar. "Here's at least one thing that's leaking into the stream!"

Alison's eyes lit up. "I can't believe it!" She reached for the jar and squinted at it. About a tablespoon of reddish dirt clung to the inside of the glass. "I mean, I hope this is what's wrecking the stream and everything."

"The air was so bad around it," I said, "I really think this is it."

Alison looked at me. "Even if it isn't, Carly, I'm never coming near here again."

"Me either!"

Then she froze. Only her eyes moved as she looked over my shoulder. "I hear something again!" she whispered.

Now I could hear noises behind me. Please let it be another deer! I slowly turned and looked, but all I could see was a bend in the stream. I put the jar in my backpack, and we crawled behind the closest bush. We knelt there holding hands and barely breathing.

The noises came closer, louder. Clump, clump, clump. Someone wearing boots.

I heard Alison swallow. "It's Joe," she said in my ear. "He finally caught us."

She's right, I thought. And we're no match for him now. I can't even run.

Clump, clump, clump, clump . . .

"I'm sorry, Alison. I didn't want this to happen."

"I know." More tears spilled down her cheeks.

Then a deep voice yelled, "Carly? Alison?"

Alison gasped.

I jumped up, pulling her with me. "It's Randy!"

I stumbled toward his voice. "Randy! We're here! Over here!"

"Where? Where are you?" Just then he ran around the bend in the stream and saw me. "Carly! I was looking for you—"

He stopped a few feet away and stared at the blood on my shirt and jeans. His face turned pale. "What happened? Did . . . did Joe find you?"

Alison walked up behind me and started to giggle. Or maybe she was crying. "We . . . we thought you were Joe . . . and that deer. . . . " She giggled again and pointed into the woods.

"A deer?" He looked at the trees where she was pointing and then turned back to me. "Carly, what happened?"

"It wasn't Joe." My voice was hoarse. "It was the stream. Randy, we found out what's polluting the stream." I hadn't even told Alison the rest yet. "And it's coming from a metal tank marked 'Faraday.'"

99

Alison inhaled sharply. "I knew it!"

"Faraday?" Randy's mouth fell open.

I pulled the jar out of my backpack and handed it to him.

"That dirt was around the tank," I told him. "Whatever was in the tank, some kind of chemical I guess, leaked out and turned the dirt red." I looked him in the eye. "Randy, I could see where the chemical was leaking right into the stream."

"Faraday?" He looked at the jar again and shook his head.

"That's what it says, right on the tank. Someone's been telling you stories at work."

"I knew it!" Alison said again.

Randy frowned and began to unscrew the lid.

"Don't!" I grabbed the jar away from him. "Don't open it!"

"Let's just go home, okay?" Alison tugged on my shirt. "I mean, the last thing I want to do is breathe more of that stuff. And I really, really want to get these clothes off and take a shower!" She reached down and tried to pull her slimy jeans away from her legs.

But Randy wasn't in any hurry. "Where did you find this dirt?"

He wanted to see the tank himself, I guessed.

"You can't breathe there, Randy," I told him.

"Honest! Look, your nose is already running from getting this close."

"Just a little." He wiped it with the back of his hand.

I held up the jar. "The air gets a lot worse where this came from. A lot worse! Let's see if we can find out what's in this dirt first. Then we can get more people and come back with gas masks or something."

Then you'll see that the tank is marked Faraday, I thought.

He looked upstream for a minute and finally nodded. "Okay, but let's hurry so we can get back here before dark."

"I mean, I'm outta here!" Alison said. She headed downstream.

But Randy kept looking upstream. I put the jar in my backpack and followed Alison, holding my breath until I heard him walking behind me. I sure didn't want him to find that ravine. If he went down there and the fumes got him, Alison and I were in no shape to pull him out.

Besides, we needed him. We had to cross the cornfield again. Maybe this time, Joe *would* be waiting for us.

Think of something else, I told myself. "I thought you had to work today, Randy."

"And miss all this fun?"

I glanced back, but he wasn't smiling. I knew he still couldn't believe Faraday had dumped chemicals in the ravine.

"I traded with one of the other guys," he said. "He couldn't come in till 1:30, so I had to work until then."

"Well, I think we should call the newspaper and everything right away, " Alison told us over her shoulder.

I shook my head. "Let's talk to Dad first, tell him what we found. He can help us find out what's in that dirt."

At least I hoped he'd help. He had to believe us now! We had proof this wasn't just Alison's imagination. Or mine.

Randy was awfully quiet now. Was he sorry he followed us out here? I turned around to ask him, but he was frowning at the ground as we walked, lost in his own thoughts.

The cornfield was still empty when we got there. Even the men working on the houses had gone home. We hurried across, heading straight for the woods on the other side instead of following the wandering stream. We were panting—but safe—by the time we reached the trees.

A few minutes later, the stream led us back to the park.

"We made it!" Alison gasped as we stopped

a minute to catch our breath. "I mean, Joe must have taken the day off or something!" We hurried through the park, which was fortunately empty, and headed for my house.

"Dad?" I called as I opened my front door.

"In here," he called from the kitchen. "I hope you're hungry. I made chili!"

I turned to Alison and Randy. "Stay here a minute, okay?" Somehow I thought I could explain better by myself.

Dad was stirring a big pot on the stove and watching the evening news on the TV. He glanced at me as I walked into the kitchen.

"Carly!" He dropped his spoon into the chili and rushed over. "Is that blood? What happened?"

"Just a nose bleed. It stopped now."

Dad pulled me closer to the light over the sink. "But you've been crying! And how did you get so sunburned?"

Sunburned? I looked down at my arms. They were bright pink. My face must be burned, too. I must look a lot like Betty now.

"I wasn't crying, Dad. It was the stream."

"The stream? You got sunburned at the stream?"

"It's not sunburn."

"Carly, would you please tell me what's going on?"

I took a deep breath, but that made me cough. "I . . . we followed the stream today, to see what was leaking into it."

"We? You and Alison again? How far did you go? What if—"

"We had to do it." Alison was standing in the doorway with Randy behind her.

Dad blinked in surprise. Then he squinted at Alison. "Alison, come over here, will you?"

He pulled her under the light. "At least you're not quite so sunburned as Carly here."

"It's *not* the sun, Dad. It's chemicals in the stream."

He tilted his head and raised one eyebrow.

I pulled the jar out of my backpack one more time. I held it while I told Dad about finding the ravine—and the tank leaking into the stream. Randy moved closer so he could hear every word.

"A tank? Leaking into the stream?" Dad asked. "How would a tank of chemicals get into a ravine? Where did it come from?"

Randy crossed his arms over his chest and waited for me to say it. Alison shifted from one foot to the other; she was bursting to tell him, but she let me.

"From Faraday Fuel, Dad."

I could see Dad's Adam's apple move as he swallowed.

"Carly saw it written right on the tank!" Alison added.

Dad stared into space for a minute. Then he turned to Alison and Randy. "Did you two see this tank with 'Faraday' on it?"

Alison shook her head. "I was, you know, trying to pull Carly out of the ravine before she . . . I mean, I didn't see it, but Carly did!"

"Pull her out?"

"The ravine walls were kind of steep, that's all." I tried to smile, but my face hurt. "I'm okay now."

"Well, you've looked better." He brushed a strand of my hair back from my face and turned to Randy. "Did you see 'Faraday' written on the tank?"

Randy shook his head. "I didn't catch up with them until they were on their way back. But we could go there right now and check it." He took a step toward the door.

The thought of going back down there made my chest hurt. "Dad, don't you think we should find out what's in this dirt before we go back? Maybe we should be taking gas masks or something. Faraday must have someone who could tell what's in here."

Dad rubbed his forehead with his fingers while he thought it over. Then he took the jar from me and held it up to the light. The dirt was in red clumps now. He pushed his lips together.

Alison couldn't stand waiting. "Well, I think we should, you know, call the news—"

I shook my head at her and she stopped. I knew the last thing Dad wanted to do was call the newspaper.

"What if . . . what if we don't say how we found it?" I suggested. "Maybe someone at Faraday would help us figure out what was in it then."

Dad didn't answer. Instead, he started to unscrew the lid.

"Oh, don't!" Alison put up her hands and backed away.

"Let him," I whispered. "Then he'll know." We huddled on the far side of the kitchen, but Randy bent closer to Dad.

The fumes seemed to rush through the kitchen like a brush fire. Dad started to choke and jammed the lid back on. Randy must have got a lungful. He stumbled into the living room and stood there holding his chest and gasping for breath.

Alison and I followed him, taking deep breaths of the living room air. I think we had both stopped breathing as soon as Dad opened the jar. Our eyes had already started to water.

Dad set the closed jar on the kitchen table

and hurried to open the front door and let fresh air in. Then he stood looking out the door with his hands on his hips, trying to catch his breath. Slowly, he pulled his handkerchief out of his pants pocket and wiped his nose and eyes. When he turned to us, he was pale.

"Faraday . . . I can't believe it." He shook his head, then moved closer and put his hands on my shoulders. "Look at you, with your bloody shirt and burned face. I hate to think of what you went through to get that dirt, Carly. If only I'd listened . . . "

He gently kissed the top of my head. "I expect you're right about Faraday's name on the tank, too. I'm sorry, baby."

Then he reached over and took Alison's hand. "Young lady, I apologize to you, too. You were right this time."

Alison nodded. But then she looked puzzled. "This time?"

"Well," Randy interrupted in a hoarse voice, "what are we going to do now?" He looked as grim as Dad. I guess it hurts to see your hero die, even if your hero is a chemical company.

Dad glanced into the kitchen, where the jar sat innocently on the table. "Let's get to the bottom of this."

Ten

DAD turned off the stove and made a quick phone call. Then he turned to Alison and Randy. "Maybe you two better call home and tell your folks where you are."

Alison smiled. "I told them I was going to, you know, eat dinner at your house."

"I think my parents went out to eat," Randy said. "They won't be home for a while."

"Then let's go." Dad herded the three of us out to the car.

"Where are we going?" I slid into the front seat beside him, cradling the jar.

"Waste Control at Faraday. Someone's there twenty-four hours a day," Dad explained. "And they better have some answers. They're lucky all that stuff did so far was give Jeremy a rash."

"I mean, that's not all, for sure!" Alison informed him as she got in the back seat with Randy.

Dad gave me a sharp look. "What else?"

I finally told him about my rash, and Cecily's—and about poor Betty with her blisters and oxygen tank. As I talked, Dad kept shaking his head and driving faster. All of a sudden, I felt real tears stinging my eyes. I never should have doubted whose side he'd be on.

"Not yet," Alison muttered to herself. I glanced back. She was holding her arms up to the window, checking for a rash, I guessed—or blisters.

"This just doesn't make sense," Randy said in a low voice. "Pete didn't make up all those things he told me."

"Pete?" Dad asked.

"My boss at the warehouse. He said Faraday knew more about handling chemicals than anyone in the business."

Alison snorted. "Yeah, they figured out how to get rid of their toxic chemicals, all right!"

"Pete wouldn't lie to me!" Randy insisted.

They argued until we got to Faraday's main gate. The guard saw the Faraday sticker on our car and waved us through. Dad turned down a narrow road between two pipes that were as big around as our car. A few minutes later, he stopped in front of a small brick building marked "Waste Control."

A tall, thin woman in a long, white lab coat

met us at the door. A plastic name tag pinned to her coat pocket said "Martin." Her hair was a cap of tight brown curls. Dark-rimmed glasses perched halfway down her nose.

"I just called," Dad told her.

She nodded at him without smiling, but when she glanced at the rest of us, she blinked in surprise. Maybe Dad should have waited for Alison and me to clean up a little.

Ms. Martin pulled her eyes away from my bloody shirt and turned back to Dad. "I'm working on a major project right now, so I only have a minute to look at whatever it is you found."

She folded her arms across her chest. "However, your suggestion that Faraday has something to do with toxic chemicals in a stream is outrageous. I understand that you've worked here a very short time, Mr. Hendricks, but you should still be aware that Faraday takes pride in its environmental awareness." Her eyes flashed. "We do not, under any conditions, discard our waste chemicals in the local waterways."

Dad looked her in the eye and handed her the jar. "I'm surprised about this, too. Let's just see what's in here."

She snatched the jar, turned, and headed down a long hallway behind her. We hurried to keep up. Her heels clicked so loudly on the tile floor it was hard to hear what she was saying.

"Believe me, I can account for every molecule of hazardous waste Faraday has produced since 1976, when the federal government passed the Resource Conservation and Recovery Act. We have to keep more records than you might think possible. I am absolutely positive that whatever you found—if it is indeed a toxic chemical—has nothing whatsoever to do with Faraday."

Alison poked me in the side and rolled her eyes.

Ms. Martin pushed through a set of swinging doors. Dad held one of the doors open for us. The room was a small laboratory. All four walls were lined with tables. The tables were crowded with microscopes, boxes of slides, and glass beakers. The rows of bright lights overhead made my eyes water. In the middle of the room, a shower head hung from the ceiling—for emergencies, I guessed. I saw a drain in the floor underneath it.

Ms. Martin stopped at the nearest table. Four beakers filled with bluish liquid had been placed in a very straight row. She held our jar up to the light and jotted something down on a clipboard lying on the table. Then she looked puzzled and sniffed gingerly at the jar.

"This is bromine! I'd recognize that smell anywhere. That proves it!" She allowed herself a small smile of triumph. The four of us just stared at her.

"Faraday doesn't use bromine any more," she said. "I haven't seen any bromine in the entire sixteen and a half years I've worked here. In fact . . . " Ms. Martin grabbed a dusty notebook off a shelf above the table and leafed through it.

Alison glanced nervously around. "This room is full of poison," she whispered in my ear.

Randy leaned over a microscope on the table and sneaked a look at a slide. Dad stood with a grim expression and his arms crossed, watching Ms. Martin.

"As these records clearly indicate," she said, jabbing her finger at a page, "the last year Faraday used any bromine was 1971. It was used in processing leaded gasoline for automobiles."

Ms. Martin gave us a frosty smile. "And, as you know, Faraday now specializes in fuel for the airline industry, processed *without* bromine. Satisfied?"

Randy let his breath out. "Well, I guess that

settles it." He took a step toward the lab door.

Alison put her hands on her hips. "But, I mean, Carly saw 'Faraday' written right on that tank!"

"Carly." Ms. Martin muttered. She looked at me. "I presume you're Carly?"

I nodded.

"And what exactly did you see?"

Dad moved closer to me. "Go ahead and tell her, honey."

My mouth was dry. "Well, we . . . I found a little metal tank at the bottom of this ravine. It was stuck in some dried-up mud, and it had 'Faraday' printed on the side."

As soon as I said it, I realized the truth. I didn't really see "Faraday" written on the tank. Just FAR. Maybe it said FARNHAM or FARAWAY, which is where I wished I were. I swallowed hard.

Ms. Martin glared at me. "This tank had 'Faraday' printed on the side? Are you absolutely positive?"

"Uh—" I wanted to tell her what I really saw, but her eyes dared me to say another word.

"Ms. Martin, I trust my daughter on this," Dad told her.

I felt the blood drain out of my face. Dad was trying to make up for not believing me before, but this time maybe I was wrong . . .

"Someone from Faraday needs to go and check that tank," Dad was saying. "Someone from Waste Control."

Ms. Martin crossed her arm. and tapped her foot. "Mr. Hendricks, I am here by myself and I have a whole night's work ahead of me. Can't this wait for the morning shift?"

Dad took my hand. "Look at my daughter," he said quietly. "Look how that bromine—or whatever it is—burned her skin."

Ms. Martin glanced sideways at me without moving her head or uncrossing her arms.

"Carly tells me all that blood on her shirt is from a nosebleed," Dad went on.

Ms. Martin pushed her lips into a thin line. "Bromine could do that," she admitted.

"So let's open the jar," he suggested. "Then we'll see if we have a problem that can wait until morning."

Alison immediately backed toward the lab doors, but Ms. Martin just stared at the jar in her hand. Then she sighed and looked at the ceiling. "Just where is this ravine?"

Dad turned to us.

Alison shrugged. "Well, you know—out in the woods!"

"It . . . it might be on the Robbinses' farm," I said. Maybe the tank did say "Faraday."

That made the most sense, didn't it?

"If that ravine is on private property, we can't very well trespass." Ms. Martin handed the jar back to Dad.

"That tank is leaking into a stream," Dad told her. "The stream runs through a park and little kids play in it. Some of them already have gotten a rash from this stuff. And it's possible that these chemicals are leaking into well water." He held up the jar.

Ms. Martin tried to stare him down, but finally she threw up her hands. "All right, all right, but I'll have to get the EPA to come with us, in case we have to go on this . . . this farm."

"The EPA!" Alison smiled. "Now we're going to get some action!"

My legs felt so rubbery I had to lean against the table. The Environmental Protection Agency was part of the government, kind of like the police! What if I was wrong? How could this be happening?

Ms. Martin looked at Dad over the tops of her glasses. "If we involve the EPA, they'll send a formal report to the top management here at Faraday. Are you absolutely positive you want that to happen?"

"Uh . . . " I had to say something! Dad was risking his job now, that was clear.

"Call them," he said. "Carly—and Alison—went through a lot to get that dirt. I'm not going to let them down now."

Alison clapped her hands. "I mean, wait till I tell all the kids at school about this!"

I tried to breathe normally. Dad trusted me. I hoped it wouldn't cost him his job.

Out of the corner of my eye, I could see Randy frowning at the floor. His job would be on the line, too, if Ms. Martin found out he worked for Faraday. If I was wrong about that tank, he'd never get to be a gofer in the engineering department.

I moved closer to him. "Maybe you should leave," I whispered. "In case this . . . this doesn't work out." I nodded toward Ms. Martin. "She doesn't even know your name yet."

Randy raised his head and looked at me. Then he reached for my hand. "I'll stay. Your dad is right." He nodded at my filthy shirt. "You've done your part. The least I can do is stay and help see this through."

I nodded and swallowed hard. Maybe the tank did say "Faraday." I hoped with all my might it did. There weren't any other chemical companies near Seaside, were there? Especially ones that started with the letters FAR?

"If that's what you want then," Ms. Martin was saying to Dad. She walked over to a cabinet and pulled out a big, lumpy canvas bag. On it was a picture that looked like a monster with bulging eyes and a snout. Gas masks.

Then another thought made me feel a little better. I was sure we needed gas masks to go back down in that ravine. That tank was full of a dangerous chemical, right? Even if maybe it wasn't from Faraday? Something still had to be done about it!

But not by Faraday, I reminded myself. And certainly not by Ms. Martin from Waste Control. If the tank didn't say Faraday, no matter how dangerous the chemical was, the rest of the people at Faraday would be just as annoyed with us as Ms. Martin was.

What did that tank say?

"You carry this." Ms. Martin dropped the bag of gas masks by Randy's feet. She motioned Alison and me toward a sink built into a lab table. "You two rinse that dirt off and use this." She pulled a tube of cream out of a drawer and tossed it to me.

The label said something about chemical burns. After I rinsed my face, the cream felt cool on my skin. Alison tried some after she saw that it didn't dissolve my face.

Then I remembered something else, a worry I had tried not to think about. I turned

117

toward Ms. Martin and cleared my throat noisily. She was putting on a pair of sneakers that were even whiter than her lab coat. She glanced up impatiently.

"Um . . . does bromine cause . . . cancer? Or something else just as bad?"

Alison dropped the tube of cream in the sink. Dad turned pale. Randy had been looking at the picture of the gas mask on the bag, but now he seemed to be carved of stone. We waited for her answer.

"Bromine?" Ms. Martin said. "No, not that I know of. But, as you proved, it's extremely caustic to the skin and respiratory system."

Just then the lab doors swung open, and two men in beige shirts and pants came in. A green patch on their sleeves said "EPA."

I took a couple of deep breaths and tried to relax. That tank had better say "Faraday."

One man's name tag said Stevenson. He had a walkie-talkie strapped to a belt that barely stretched around his stomach.

The other one, Buckner, was taller and had a thin mustache. He was carrying a clipboard. "Got a problem here?"

"Probably not," Ms. Martin muttered.

"How did you get here so fast?" Randy blurted out.

Stevenson glanced at Ms. Martin in

surprise. "Didn't she tell you? We've been here all afternoon, making our regular inspection."

I could see Ms. Martin was trying to make this even scarier than it had to be.

"Let's just get this over with," she snapped.

The men eyed my bloody shirt while Dad explained how Alison and I had found the tank. At first Buckner took notes, but then he stopped writing and put his clipboard under his arm. When Dad finished, Buckner and Stevenson exchanged a knowing look.

They didn't believe us. I didn't blame them. I wasn't sure I believed us.

Buckner turned to Alison and me. "How old are you?"

"I mean, what difference does it make?" Alison's face was red, but it wasn't because of the bromine. "How old do you have to be before the EPA, you know, protects you?"

Buckner held his hands up. "Now wait a minute, Miss—"

Dad stepped between them. "Can we just find that ravine and take a look at the tank?"

A few minutes later, we left. Dad, Alison, Randy, and I led the way in our car. Ms. Martin rode with the men in a beige EPA van. I was glad I couldn't hear what she was telling them.

We were heading for the park when Randy

119

yelled, "There! That's the cornfield!" He was pointing between two half-built houses. "The ravine's in those woods back there!"

Dad glanced at me. I shrugged. It did look familiar.

We stopped in front of the houses, and the EPA van pulled up behind us. Soon we were all picking our way across the rutted field toward the trees. Dad carried the bag of gas masks. Buckner had a different measuring instrument in each hand, and Stevenson was lugging a case marked "Specimen Kit."

We spotted the stream snaking across the field and followed it into the woods. Randy went first, with me, Alison, Dad, and the other adults following single file.

A few minutes later, my eyes started to burn again. I heard Dad blow his nose.

"Good thing you brought those masks," Buckner told Ms. Martin.

Alison snickered behind me and leaned closer. "I mean, what a baby!" she whispered.

For the next five minutes, no one talked, but there was plenty of sniffling and coughing. I wiped my face on the last clean patch of my shirt and glanced back at the adults. Dad's eyes were watery, but he gave me a thumbs-up sign and shifted the bag of masks to his other shoulder.

I crossed my fingers tighter. If I were wrong about that tank, it would only be fair that he never trusted me again.

Ms. Martin glared at the ground as she picked her way along the bank. Every few steps, she patted her eyes with a tissue.

"Time for the masks," Buckner called out.

We stopped and opened the bag. Four masks for seven of us.

"I don't need one, anyway," Alison said. "I mean, I already saw the ravine. You see one, you've seen them all." She grinned and wiped her face with the back of her hand.

"I want to wear one," I told Buckner. "I can show you where the tank is." And, I thought, see what it says, the sooner, the better. Right now I felt as if I had a lump of bromine in my stomach, eating away my insides.

"No," Dad said in that quiet voice he always used when I was supposed to stop arguing. "Four masks, four adults."

"But . . . ," Randy objected.

No one paid him any attention. Dad, Ms. Martin, and the two men put on the masks. Buckner had to help Dad with his.

Alison giggled. They looked like they just stepped off a flying saucer—or out of a horror movie—but my stomach hurt too much to laugh.

They headed farther upstream and left Randy, Alison, and me standing beside the empty bag. Stevenson was still carrying the specimen case, and Buckner had his gauges.

"Stay here," Dad had said in his sternest voice.

How could I? I had to watch them from the top of the ravine. Once they dug up that tank, I'd see for sure what was written on it. And Dad would find out—maybe too late—whether he was wrong to trust me.

Eleven

R ANDY came with me. We stayed back a
 ways so the adults wouldn't know we
were following them, but with those gas
masks on, I don't think they could have heard
elephants coming. The hardest part was getting close to that ravine again. The fumes
seemed to get stronger with every step we
took.

We crouched behind some bushes by the
hill and watched Dad and the others struggle
to the top. They looked like giant ants with
clothes on. But even Ms. Martin went over
the edge. I guess she wanted to see that tank
as much as I did.

As soon as they were out of sight, Randy
and I crawled up the hill and lay side by side
at the top, peeking over the edge and breathing as shallowly as possible.

"I sure wish I had one of those masks." My

throat was raw from the first trip, and the air burned worse than before.

"I still can't believe Faraday did this," Randy whispered hoarsely. He wiped his face on the shoulder of his shirt.

The group below was moving toward the tank. I saw a flash of light, but it was only Buckner taking pictures. Stevenson was pointing out the rusty barrels in the mound of trash.

They stopped in a semi-circle around the half-buried tank. I swallowed to keep from throwing up. It had better say "Faraday."

Stevenson pushed a long stick under the tank and pried it out of the mud. Just then Ms. Martin stepped closer and blocked my view! Without thinking, I stood up.

Randy yanked me back down. "They'll see us!"

Then Ms. Martin moved again and I could see the tank.

FARADAY. Relief washed over me. *It really did say "Faraday."*

Stevenson was packing reddish dirt from around the tank into jars from the specimen case. Ms. Martin had retreated to the wall of the ravine, right below us. I was tempted to start a landslide and bury her, but I wanted to hear her explain how Faraday chemicals got into this ravine.

"They're coming up!" Randy grabbed my arm and we slid down the hill. We stumbled along the bank of the stream, taking deep breaths of the cleaner air. My eyes were watering so much it was hard to see.

"Did they find it?" Alison called as we came into sight.

I nodded. My throat hurt too much to talk.

Randy was bent over with his hands on his thighs, trying to catch his breath. Alison patted his back. "Are you okay and everything? I mean, it's really bad up there, isn't it?"

He closed his eyes. I had a feeling his throat and chest didn't hurt nearly as much as his heart. Randy had been so proud to work at Faraday.

We heard the adults coughing before we saw them. They were carrying the gas masks and looking grim. Buckner trailed behind them, dipping his gauges into the stream every so often and writing something on a clipboard. Then he put his equipment down and tacked a sign to a tree:

Contaminated Land
KEEP OFF
By Order of the EPA

"At last!" Alison whispered.

The sign gave me goosebumps. I edged away from the stream.

Ms. Martin had dirty streaks on her lab coat and sneakers, but she hadn't given up. "I'll say it again: No one from Faraday Fuel put that tank there."

"But it was there! And it was marked Faraday!" Dad said.

"I think she's right," Stevenson said. "Faraday *didn't* put that tank there—or all that garbage. Someone else used that ravine as a dump."

As he talked, he filled a small jar and a quart container with water from the stream. Then he wrote "3" on both labels and used a huge black marker to put another "3" on a tree nearby.

Alison nodded. "Taking water samples—I mean, that's good!"

Stevenson smiled a little. "I'm glad you think so." He turned to Dad and Ms. Martin. "First thing in the morning, we'll have people come in and go through that trash. No telling what else is there."

"But what about the stream?" Randy asked.

"We'll have to get these water samples checked in the lab before we decide about that." Stevenson looked at me. "Whose farm did you say this property might be on?"

"Joe and Betty Robbins," I told him.

"Well, let's go talk to them," Buckner said.

A few minutes later, the car and the EPA van bounced up the driveway to the Robbinses' old farmhouse. My heart dropped when I saw the red pickup outside.

"He's here." Alison whispered. She sounded as if she were strangling.

Everyone got out of the vehicles and climbed the creaky steps onto the front porch.

"Alison, do you think—" I turned, but she had vanished. It took me a minute to spot her. She'd climbed back into our car, and was huddling in the back seat, her face pale. She gave me a little wave. Alison wasn't taking any chances being near Joe.

"I can smell the bromine here," Ms. Martin muttered. She held a once-clean tissue over her mouth.

Buckner nodded. "Must have seeped into their well water."

Just as Alison and I had guessed!

Stevenson knocked on the frame of the rickety screen door. "Anyone home?"

I could hear the wheels on Betty's cart squeaking as she shuffled toward the door.

"Who . . . who is it?" She peered out the rusty screen.

Stevenson gasped. Betty's face certainly

127

hadn't healed since the last time I'd been here.

Buckner cleared his throat. "We're from the EPA, ma'am."

"Who's out there?" yelled a scratchy voice behind Betty. Then Joe stepped in front of Betty and pushed open the door. It was a good thing Alison had waited in the car. The blisters on his face were pink and raw, nestled among his whiskers. I could see why he hadn't shaved in a while. His eyes seemed to peer at us from deep red holes.

Joe coughed once and spit something in the front yard. I glanced away.

"We're from the EPA," said Buckner in an official voice. "We want to talk to you about some dumping on what we believe is your land."

Joe scratched a spot on his forehead. "Dumping?" he asked hoarsely.

Buckner nodded. "Yes, sir. Someone's been dumping in a ravine that may be on your land."

Betty gasped. "Oh, Joe, that's . . . that's where—"

Joe silenced his sister with a sharp look. Then he held up a red and blistered hand. "Look, I don't know if you college guys can tell time or not, but it's pretty late."

Darkness was swiftly falling. I blinked, astonished at how much time had passed.

"We was about to turn in," Joe growled. He started to close the screen door.

Buckner stopped the door with his foot. "Sir, do you know who dumped some barrels and at least one small metal tank in that ravine? They might be making you and your sister sick."

Joe frowned and came out on the porch. "What are you talking about? Why, there wasn't nothing bad in them barrels. . . . "

Joe *knew* the barrels were there!

Buckner raised his chin. "Mr. Robbins, at least one of those containers has some dangerous chemicals in it. We're going to get it out of the ravine as soon as possible, but we have to know how it got there in the first place."

Betty shuffled out the door and stood beside her brother. Her breathing seemed to get more ragged by the second. She started patting her chest. The kitten came out and rubbed against her leg.

Joe put his hands in his back pockets and stared over the porch rail into the growing darkness. "Heck, I didn't do nothing wrong. And anyway, no one ever went near that ravine. I ain't been there m'self in years. I can't see as what the problem is now." He turned to go back into the house.

Ms. Martin stepped into his path. "You dumped those barrels there yourself! You must have stolen them from Faraday!"

"Stole them?" Joe hooted. "Not hardly! Faraday paid me good money to take them away!"

We all stared at him. Faraday *did* dump them!

"Joe . . . " Betty coughed. "Joe was just trying to keep our farm together. That was the summer . . . the summer of 1970. I remember because it never rained and our corn crop dried up. Faraday needed some . . . barrels trucked away, and we . . . we needed the money. . . . " She coughed again. "Joe didn't mean any harm."

Gently, I put an arm around Betty's thin shoulders. "Chemicals from those barrels are leaking into your well water. That's why your skin . . . " I couldn't say it.

Ms. Martin could. "Bromine fumes from one of those containers are burning holes in your skin and probably in your lungs."

"You can't live here any longer," Buckner added. "This farmhouse will have to be condemned, probably torn down."

Suddenly Betty sagged against me.

"She's fainted!" Dad said. He and Buckner

gingerly picked Betty up and laid her on the porch swing.

Stevenson unhooked the walkie-talkie from his belt and called for an ambulance. Joe hovered over his sister, patting her hand. He was pale under his burned skin. None of us said much while we waited for help.

Just as Betty opened her eyes, the ambulance roared up the driveway. The paramedics strapped an oxygen mask over her face and bundled her onto a stretcher. Joe insisted on walking to the ambulance, but Dad and Stevenson stayed beside him and caught him when his legs started to fold. Joe seemed years older than he had a few minutes ago.

Alison had crept out of hiding when the ambulance showed up. Now we all watched as the ambulance dodged the deepest holes in the driveway and sped to the hospital.

Ms. Martin turned to us. "I . . . I can see now how this happened." Her voice was softer now, and it cracked a couple of times. "Years ago, when Faraday did use bromine, there were no laws to control toxic waste. Few people realized what it could do. I'm sure hiring Joe to take away those barrels was simply a matter of . . . well, cleaning up a warehouse."

Buckner nodded. "True. And it'll be years

before we find all the old dumps like this that everyone's forgotten about."

Ms. Martin looked at me and Alison with sad eyes. "But if you girls find another one of these dumps, call me. This scares me, too. I'll make sure people listen instead of giving you a hard time." She patted my arm. "Congratulations. It took courage to see this through."

Buckner offered Ms. Martin a ride back to Faraday. I scooped up Betty's kitten and followed Dad back to our car. I kept thinking about what Ms. Martin said as we drove to Alison's house. She thought I had courage!

Alison's parents stood in their kitchen with their mouths open while Alison told them what we had found. They kept glancing at Dad, expecting him to say it wasn't true, I guess, but he just nodded.

" . . . and then Mr. Hendricks drove us here." Alison reached for the phone. "I mean, who should we call first, the newspaper or the TV station?"

"Now wait a minute, Alison," her mom said.

"Mom!" she protested. "Carly and I risked our lives for this, you know—"

"Uh, Alison," Dad said. "We need to think about this. The EPA is probably calling the execs at Faraday right now. We have to give them a chance to find out what's going on before reporters show up. It's only fair."

Alison rolled her eyes.

"Why don't we wait till morning, okay?" Dad asked. "I'll call you first thing tomorrow to tell you what's happening."

She made a face. "Okay, I guess I can wait that long." She turned to me and grinned. "I bet that when people find out what we did, some reporters will come and talk to us. Let's, you know, wear these same clothes, right? I mean, in case they bring their cameras and everything?"

My shirt felt cold and clammy against my skin. "Uh, I have to watch Jeremy in the morning." I didn't want my picture taken, not even in clean clothes. "Go ahead without me."

"You're going to miss the best part!" Her eyes sparkled.

Dad and I took Randy home, but he didn't want us to come in with him. "I'll tell my parents myself."

I wondered if he would. I didn't think so, at least not tonight, not until he got things sorted out in his mind.

After I took a shower and got in bed, I couldn't sleep. I had too many things to sort out myself. How would I tell Ginny? Would her park be condemned, too?

Twelve

WHEN I rang the Newmans' doorbell at 7:30 the next morning, Jeremy opened the door. His big blue eyes were full of worry.

"Mommy's crying."

Uh-oh. I followed him into the kitchen, where Ginny was on the phone.

"The Robbinses' farm? Oh, Brian!"

Brian Haynes, mayor of Seaside. Ginny was blotting tears off her face with a napkin. "Call me at the office when you know more, okay?"

As she hung up, she turned and saw me. "Oh, Carly, you're never going to believe this! That stream is polluted! The one that goes through the park! The one Jeremy plays in! What if that water hurt him somehow?"

She lifted his chin with her hand and looked into his eyes. "Are you okay, honey? You're not sick, are you?"

"I'm okay, Mommy. Don't be sad." He hugged her neck.

"You don't have to worry," I told her. "The stream just gave him that rash—and made his nose run."

"The stream did that?" She frowned. "How do you know? Anyway, his rash is almost gone now."

She unwrapped him from her neck and held out one of his arms. I could barely see pink dots on the inside of his elbow.

"Maybe the pollution is gone, too! I bet the mayor is worried about nothing. The park is safe! Everything's okay!"

I shook my head. "I haven't let Jeremy go near that water all week. That's why he's better."

She looked bewildered. "I . . . that's good . . . I mean, thank goodness you kept him out of it!" She hugged Jeremy. "But then, maybe the stream is still . . . "

She finally looked closely at me. "Carly, is that sunburn?"

At least I wasn't still wearing the bloody shirt. "No, it was the stream." I finally told her the whole story. She was pale by the time I finished. Jeremy had squirmed away and run off to watch cartoons.

"I wish I had known all this before, Carly."

"Maybe I should have told you," I admitted. "But Alison and I weren't sure, not till last night. I thought you had enough problems to worry about. I made sure Jeremy was safe, though, as soon as we guessed it was the stream."

"I know you did, honey. I owe you a lot for that." She pulled me close and hugged me. "You're going to be a good mother some day, Carly."

Now there were tears in my eyes, too.

"At least Brian says we might be able to keep the park open," Ginny told me. "The EPA has already seen to getting a fence put up between the park and the stream, to keep kids out of the water."

Ginny shook her head and headed for the bathroom. "I've got to fix my face and get over to my office. But I don't know how I'll concentrate on selling houses today."

She'd been gone only a few minutes when Randy rang the doorbell.

"I know it's still early, but I, well, I had to see how you're doing," he said.

Pleased, I blushed slightly. "Well, I'm glad we found out the truth about the stream. And I'm glad Ginny finally knows. And I'm really glad I helped Betty, even if you thought I couldn't." I had to smile.

"I underestimated you, I admit it!" Randy grinned and held up his hands in surrender.

Just then the phone rang. As soon as I picked it up, Alison shouted, "Turn the TV on! Quick! Quick! Channel 4!"

I ran into the family room and switched from Jeremy's cartoons to Channel 4.

"Hey!" Jeremy yelled. But then he looked at the screen with Randy and me. "The park!"

And so it was. A reporter with a microphone and a man in a suit were standing in front of a new metal fence that was taller than they were. I gaped, astonished at how quickly the fence had been erected. It stretched across the back of the park and glittered in the morning sun. Pieces of sod lay on the grass where holes had hurriedly been dug for fence posts. Every few feet along the fence, signs warned "Contaminated Land—KEEP OUT—By Order of the EPA."

A shiver went up my back.

"Why is that fence there, Carly?" Jeremy asked.

I put my finger to my lips. "I'll tell you in a minute."

Now the camera turned to show two more people standing nearby—Mayor Haynes and Buckner, who looked tired, but much neater than he had last night. In the background, a crowd stood quietly by the park swings, watching to see what would happen.

The man in the suit was apparently from Faraday, and he was talking into the reporter's microphone. "Faraday has already agreed to pay for cleaning up the dump site . . . "

The reporter didn't wait for the rest of his speech. He turned to Buckner. "Will the EPA press charges against Faraday?"

Buckner shook his head. "Not unless we find evidence that Faraday dumped those barrels after 1976. That's when the law controlling the disposal of hazardous chemicals was passed. So far, there's no sign of that."

"And Joe Robbins?" the reporter asked. "Will you charge him?"

I hadn't thought of that. Would they put old Joe in jail?

Buckner shook his head again. "He didn't break any laws at the time."

The reporter faced the camera. "And that's all we know for now. The EPA is still doing tests, but they believe the park is safe if you stay away from the stream."

Randy and I were still trying to explain things to Jeremy when Alison burst in the front door, breathlessly waving a tape of the news show.

The four of us watched the tape five or six

times. "I mean, what a bummer!" Alison complained. "They didn't even interview the real heroes, you know!"

But when the phone rang a little later, it was Alison's mother, warning us that a van of TV reporters was on its way to Jeremy's house!

"I'm outta here." Randy jumped up and headed for the back door. "See you later, heroes!" He grinned and waved as he left.

I was tempted to go with him, but I couldn't very well leave Jeremy. The next hour was a blur of questions and TV cameras. It was a good thing the reporters had another assignment or Alison would have kept them there all day.

They were starting to pack up their equipment when Ginny pulled in the driveway. She opened the car door and out jumped Freckles! The little dog spotted Jeremy and raced into his arms.

"Freckles! Freckles!" he yelled. He buried his face in the excited puppy's fur as the mini-cams hummed once more.

Ginny turned to me and smiled. "Something tells me it'll be much easier explaining to Jeremy why Freckles is back than it was explaining why she had to leave."

I smiled back, glad it wasn't me who had

to explain anything else to anyone else.

"Anyway," Ginny continued, "I decided to take the morning off. It turned out not to be a very good day for selling houses."

We talked for little longer, and then I went home. I was feeding Sweetie when Dad showed up!

"Isn't *anybody* working today?" I asked.

"Not many people at Faraday, I'll tell you." He hugged me. "This morning about half the people in the company either came to my office or called. Most of them asked how I got such a brave daughter."

"They did?" That was a lot better than what they might have asked if that tank had said FARNHAM.

Dad nodded. "And now, brave daughter, would you like to go with me to the hospital?"

"The hospital?"

"To see Betty and Joe. We are Faraday's official representatives." Then he smiled.

For a second, I wondered if Dad was keeping a secret from me. Nah, I told myself, there aren't any secrets left, thank goodness.

At the hospital, a nurse stopped us in the hallway near Betty's room. "Aren't you one of the girls who was on TV this morning? The quieter one?"

My face started to burn. "I guess."

She smiled. "I'll bet you're here to see Betty and Joe Robbins."

I nodded. "Are they going to be well soon?"

"Not well, but better. They have serious skin and respiratory damage. But at least now it won't get any worse."

Joe was sitting in a chair by Betty's bed when we walked in. Her thin body barely made a lump under her blanket. She had an oxygen tube under her nose again, and both of them had some kind of cream on their faces and arms.

"This is Carly and I'm her father," Dad told them. "We were at your house last night." He still didn't know I'd been to visit Betty earlier.

Joe turned away and stared out the window, but Betty smiled at me.

"I work at Faraday Fuel," Dad went on. "The people at Faraday feel very bad this happened, so we've made arrangements for both of you to live in a retirement center after you're well enough to leave the hospital."

I gasped. Dad winked at me. He had been keeping a secret after all! Faraday had a heart!

"Well, I'm not going!" Joe grumbled. "I'd rather be put in a cemetery than a . . . a nursing home."

"This isn't a nursing home," Dad assured

141

him. "You'll have your own apartment. It has two bedrooms and they even allow cats!"

"Sweetie . . . " Betty's eyes sparkled with tears, but she was smiling. "I hate . . . I hate to leave the farm. I was born . . . in a bedroom upstairs. But I'm so sick . . . " She patted her chest.

Joe looked at her. "I'm real sorry, Betty. I didn't know . . . "

She reached out and patted his hand.

Dad caught my eye and nodded at the door. We tiptoed out and took the elevator down to the lobby.

I couldn't get over what Dad had said. "Faraday is going to pay for an apartment for them?"

He nodded. "The execs needed a little convincing at first."

"And you did it?"

"Well, Margaret did most of it." That funny smile was back.

"Who's Margaret?"

"Um . . . Ms. Martin."

Was he blushing? What was going on here? Did Dad have another secret? "Dad, is there something I should know about?" I teased.

He stopped walking and took my hand. "Just that I'm very, very proud of you. And so is Margaret." He seemed to be trying not to smile. "In fact, she asked us to come to her house for dinner on Friday."

I grinned. "Are you sure she wants me there?"

"Well, of course, Carly—you're the hero of this whole thing. Anyway, her daughter will be there, too."

"Ms. Martin has a daughter?"

He nodded. "Margaret is divorced. Her daughter's a lot younger than you—about six, I guess. Margaret mentioned that she's very quiet. In fact, I think she doesn't talk at all."

"Not at all?" Why would a six-year-old not talk?

Maybe Alison would have some ideas. I couldn't wait to ask her.

About the Author

Linda Barr lives in a house that has a stream running through the backyard. Her son spent a summer working for the Environmental Protection Agency (testing water in local lakes and streams), her daughter is concerned about the environment, and her husband works for a company that makes chemicals, among other products. Still, she insists that none of this had anything to do with *The Secret of Seaside*.

"I noticed how much young people, including my own kids, were beginning to care about the environment," she says. "So I decided to write a story that would encourage them to get involved—and warn them about some of the real hazards out there."

This is the author's sixth novel published by Willowisp Press. She lives in Columbus, Ohio, with her husband Tom, son Dan, daughter Colleen, and a parrot named Kermit.